MARTYRS BONES

ORDER OF THADDEUS • SHORT STORY COLLECTION 2

J. A. BOUMA

INTRODUCTION

Before I was a fiction writer spinning religious conspiracy yarns, I was an evangelical Protestant pastor. I went to a former Baptist seminary turned non-denominational. Before that I was part of a ministry by a Presbyterian pastor, while attending an Episcopal Church, after attending a Baptist college recommended to me by a friend from my childhood fundamentalist Bible church.

So I've been around the ecclesiastical block, and the Protestant one at that! Given my pedigree, you could say I'm a Protestant's Protestant.

Which means things like relics are something I'm not supposed to fancy.

Yet my stories definitely reference them. The first major fiction thriller tale I wrote featured the Shroud of Turin. Definitely not Protestant. Very Catholic. And the religious order at the heart of solving that conspiracy is definitely in the non-Protestant vein of Christian things.

The Order of Thaddeus was envisioned as a Vatican-run initiative that turned into a more ecumenical Christian champion of the faith. It came out of my passion project for retrieving the vintage Christian faith and preserving it like the

Apostle Jude exhorted Christians to contend for the once-for-all faith. Along the way, I've grown in my appreciation of memory markers. Those objects that preserve the memory of Christianity.

Like the body and blood of Christ. The Eucharist, in some circles; the Lord's Supper in mine. Preserving the memory of Jesus' death on the cross for the sins of the world, paying our price in our place by suffering in the flesh and pouring out his blood.

The Shroud of Turin would be another of those memory markers, the one featured in my first Order of Thaddeus book, *Holy Shroud*, preserving the memory of Jesus' physical, bodily resurrection from the dead. Of course, that one launched this whole thing to begin with, leading to other memory markers like the Ark of the Covenant and mythical Holy Grail, even the Nicene Creed, though in a different way.

Martyrs bones are another way the Church has marked out the memory of the faith. In the extreme, such relics are venerated in a way that border on idolatry, which I have witnessed in some of my travels to overseas cathedrals. But in the healthy sense, they preserve vital inspiration and insight into the Christian faith. We remember Christ's death through the communion elements; we recall his resurrection through the Shroud of Turin, the truth of it and the hope it brings for us and our eternal life. And we can recall the great cloud of witnesses, as Hebrews 12 remarks, and all that cloud offers us by marking out the memory of our brothers and sisters in the faith—their commitment and their faithfulness, their tenacity and perseverance.

That's what I hope this collection of five original short stories accomplishes from the four Order characters we've all grown to love. In some small way, my hope is to recapture the memory of the Cloud, to mark it out through the bones of

Christians who were martyred for their faith in Christ, offering us all a worthy example of faith.

The collection opens with Silas Grey, venerating a special exhibit of Saint Peter's bone relics that connect to an interesting part of historical relations between two branches of the Church: Roman Catholicism and Eastern Orthodoxy. I thank Ed, one of my readers, for cluing me into this interesting historical nugget.

The second story connects again to history: a rather remarkable heist of a relic that has gone unsolved for years—until Celeste Bourne takes the reins! And finds herself face-to-face with an unexpected person from her past. I've fictionalized parts of it, but the underlying recent history surrounding the theft of Saint Polycarp's relics is real.

Story three gets us closer to the memory markers surrounding Jesus with Matt Gapinski's veneration of a set of apostle relics. Former tax collector Levi, known as Matthew. It's a painful anniversary, and Silas suggests he takes a break in Northern Italy to process his past. From there, things get worse —always something, right?—and he ends up saving the day.

Naomi Torres brings us our fourth story, where she is at a dig site uncovering the bones of a pair of women martyrs not enough people in the Church know about—I sure didn't, much to my chagrin. Perpetua and Felicity were two women who stood firm in their faith unto the end, even when they were threatened with a beastly death. Torres stands firm, too, when an ancient threat re-emerges headlined by a new face.

Story five brings the crew together in a final story fitting of the Order of Thaddeus series. Silas leads Celeste and Gapinski in an unusual relic hunt: digging up the bones of a Protestant Reformer. William Tyndale, the Father of the English Bible. Probably channeled my own personal background with that last one, but also believe the man's memory should be remembered—one that is nearly disrupted by a long-time, returning character.

When held in proper esteem, relics can be useful for preserving the memory of the faith. May these stories mark those memories, while giving you an entertaining, thrilling ride along the way.

Grace and peace,

~J. A. Bouma (April, 2021)

BONES OF THE ROCK

Nothing like a nighttime stroll through Embassy Row to clear the head and get the blood flowing. Especially with a clear black sky full of stars and a gentle breeze twirling around the scents of early summer, with most of DC either working or partying hard in the distant blocks around Dupont Circle.

Honking flared up from behind, followed by cheers and loud music and laughter. Probably some of the spoiled-brat embassy teenagers out hot rodding for the night. Curry followed by a mint-saffron mix and roasted goat quickly snapped my attention forward. Again, probably thanks to those very same embassies and their resident chefs cooking a mean dish for their diplomatic retinues.

Once upon a time, I'd thought about a career in the Foreign Service. Mostly because of Tom Clancy, and the data guy who seemed to have a whole lot of fun. Wasn't the State Department, but after Iraq I figured my experience abroad in the heat of battle would do the diplomats some good. But once I learned I would probably start off in some backwater banana republic no one's ever heard of, where running water and toilet paper were iffy, I figured the academy was more my style.

And seeing Silas Grey in the lights of academic papers and awards was more my style anyway.

Was almost at the end of the main drag, having passed the embassies for Korea, Japan, and Turkey. Brazil was coming up on my left, then South Africa, finishing off with the British Embassy before the massive circle that would take me past the Naval Observatory and Vice President's house on toward destiny.

Which ordinarily would have been back to the farm, the headquarters to the Order of Thaddeus under the Washington National Cathedral. The work of Order Master was never finished when the sun set, especially since I had been doing some repair work with some of the higher-ups on the Order board of directors.

More like ass-kissing work is what it was. Victor Zarruq, my handler with the board who had been a former archbishop of Libya and really was just looking out for my best interests, had urged me to tone it down a bit. By "tone it down" he meant avoid the unnecessary car chases and shoot-outs, the brute-force internet attacks and high-explosive—well, explosions and other general mayhem that was typical of SEPIO of late.

Told him it wasn't my fault an ancient threat from the shadows of the Church's history had reared its ugly head, and that a rival to that Nous beast had joined the party to give them and us a run for our religious money. Couldn't help it in the slightest. It wasn't that I went seeking those terrorist ne'er-do-wells. They found me! Well, sort of...Had to admit I did sorta dig slipping into the role of Jack Ryan from time to time.

Regardless, I was told to lie low. To refrain from sticking my head above the parapet, in his words. Which meant desk duty for a while.

Fine by me. Which meant I should have been hustling back to my study to write some more emails and put the finishing touches on some research into the cultural origins of the

Genesis narrative, believing it to be more theological propaganda given the surrounding primitive origin narratives of the day. But not tonight.

This night I was making a special appearance on behalf of the Order at an Orthodox Cathedral just down the block from HQ. Figured I'd dust off my suit and leather loafers and resurrect the old diplomatic interest, playing the part of Order envoy for the night.

Unfortunately, I was playing alone.

Tried cajoling Celeste to join me, but her mother was in town, and I'd rather steer clear of the future mom-in-law as much as possible. It's not that we didn't get along. It's that when the pair of them were together, things got...interesting. Usually with me playing interference for Celeste and then later trying to talk her off a ledge after some snide remark dear mother had laid into Celeste. So, yeah, no thanks on that.

Gapinski would have come, but apparently had a hot date thanks to SingleMingles. Thought I caught him, too, down in Dupont Circle while I was eating alone with a plate of veal parmesan and the day's *Washington Post*. Torres was on assignment overseas at a dig site that looked promising. A newly uncovered early-century something that looked like it might belong to one of the oldest churches to date.

So that left me, Master of the Order of Thaddeus, to represent at the Feast of Saint Peter at a special service just up the road from the Order's HQ at Saint Nicholas Orthodox Cathedral. They were displaying a prized possession of the Orthodox Church thanks to the generous gifting of said prize by Pope Francis a year ago.

The relics of Saint Peter himself.

Not the whole kit and caboodle, but nine fragments from the main lot that had been recovered in the late 1960s.

As a former professor who had made a name for himself in the burgeoning field of relicology, I was giddy with excitement at the prospects of laying my eyes on the bones of the Church's rock.

Was working up a sweat now, so I slowed my pace. Didn't want to ruin the suit or the shoes before arrival.

Taking a breath and passing a pair of joggers, my thoughts drifted to the man who got me into the whole relics business to begin with: Dr. Henry Gregory. A long-time family friend who had served in Vietnam with my father, and then died in that chapel at Georgetown University at the hands of terrorists that fateful day—the one that almost ended my own life had it not been for the Order. The man had become something of a second father when Dad died on 9/11. He eventually took on the role of an academic mentor when I studied under him during my doctoral work at Harvard, studying historical theology and church history.

Henry had taken an early interest in my academic career, bringing me in as his teaching aide and research assistant. Like me, the man was also a Catholic-turned-Protestant, though for different reasons. I more fell into it, though I wouldn't consider myself an ex-Catholic by any means. Just a Christian, really. Someone who came back to the faith of my childhood thanks to a Protestant evangelistic meeting in an on-base chapel back in Iraq. Henry had a later-in-life falling out after the revelations of a massive sexual abuse scandal broke in the early 2000s.

As one of the foremost experts on the emerging field of reli-cology, the study and research of historical religious relics, he taught me everything he knew about early Christian religious artifacts and their significance for the Church. Which led me to my own relic passion project, the Shroud of Turin, the cloth believed to be the burial garment of Jesus Christ of Nazareth— and the most significant Christian religious artifact. Which, now that I thought of it, led me to my current lot in life hustling down Massachusetts Ave to venerate the bones of Saint Peter!

Sometimes I wish I still had that former life. The one where

I was a former professor at Princeton, working on my latest research into the latest relic. Certainly put me in far less peril! But I also relished the opportunity to inspire a new generation to rediscover faith in the face of a modern world that rejected it as a delusion, the ravings of madmen, an opiate for the naïve masses. And I did it in a way that would make the original Protestant holder of my department office, J. Gresham Machen, turn over in his grave: through relics.

My "History of Religious Relics" class had been the most popular elective in the Department of Religion. Indiana Jones probably had something to do with that. As did Dan Brown, having popularized relics after wrapping them in the garb of religious conspiracies. I also guessed the experiential nature of religious objects of veneration also made the topic inviting.

Gone were the days when any of the religious faiths could justify themselves purely on tradition alone. Personal experiences, not dogmatic beliefs, ruled the day. And the relics from every religion offered interested students—from the committed Christian to the spiritual-but-not-religious type—the chance to explore their spiritual questions through objects rooted in historical experience.

As an academic, I had spent the majority of my research probing these objects and plumbing the depths of their history. As a Christian, I was interested in connecting historical objects of Christianity to my faith in a way that enhanced and propelled it forward.

Which was remarkable, considering Protestants dismissed such things as fanciful spiritualism at best and gross idolatry at worst. I often thought it was the inner Catholic convert rearing its head. Or maybe it was an extension of my own longing for more tangible ways to experience the God I had been searching for my whole life. Maybe still, it came from my interest in helping my students find faith, to discover what I myself had discovered in that chapel service in the middle of the Iraqi desert.

Regardless, my research had led me down interesting paths. Even made something of a name for myself in my young, blossoming career as one of the leading experts in relicology. Especially after certain events allowed me to authenticate the veracity of the Holy Shroud and scientifically prove Jesus rose from the dead. Or at least prove something monumental happened in what is believed to be Christ's tomb, preserved within the Church of the Holy Sepulchre.

Boy, did that seem like a lifetime ago.

I rounded the Naval Observatory and slowed my pace even more, lights gleaming off from the Orthodox cathedral up ahead. I could see a line of people streaming inside, and a fair amount of polished black Lincoln Town Cars dropping people off. Surely dignitaries of various stripes coming to pay the same respects I was—in my ill-fitting suit with well-worn black Johnston & Murphy sale specials. At least I was wearing a tasteful blue-patterned Zenga tie. That should count for something.

I arrived just as the last of the queue was trundling up a long set of concrete stairs and through a pair of tall walnut doors with black-iron ribbings, flanked by lights with awful fluorescent white bulbs. Hated those kinds of lights back in Princeton, and used floor lamps with yellow incandescents instead. But the light did set the white limestone facade starkly against the darkened neighborhood. The cathedral's face soared four stories with a trio of humps typical of the Orthodox architecture after which it was patterned: a 12th-century cathedral in Russia.

Towering cherry blossom trees in full bloom flanked the bulbous architecture of white limestone, throwing off their welcoming sweet scent that surly bespoke heaven itself. Bells were ringing, beckoning the faithful and faithless alike to taste and see the goodness of the Lord. I didn't mind if I did.

I made up the rear of the train of venerators, feeling inappropriately late to the party given my role within ecclesiastical circles. Taking the stairs by two, all feelings of embarrassment were drained away by the sight I beheld.

It was like walking into Alice's wonderland, it was so magnificently colorful. In the 1990s, the parish decided to renovate the interior of the cathedral by adorning it with iconic wall paintings, covering every inch of the vast space with biblical scenes and saints in magnificent colors. It was simply magical! Had never visited the church before, and now regretted not having done so for the simple visual stimulation that set my very soul soaring with upward worship.

The floor was a beautiful chocolate-white marble that covered the main nave running across east and west. A polished gold chandelier with twenty-five or thirty candles hung at the center. Above was Christ the Giver of Life, set high in the dome and looking down with love, his bronze face set against a gold backdrop and draped across him by an azure sash that matched the rest of the color scheme—a similar sky blue accenting the main arches filled with angels and cherub, apostles and saints of various stripes. It was truly breathtaking.

A perfect picture of heaven. Full of light and life, the cloud of witnesses all gathered to observe the worship, and perhaps join in the fun as well.

The nave itself was rather cramped. Not the vast space of the cathedral that housed my farm of faith defenders underneath, but that was alright. The National Cathedral was a cold, dark place with little light, zero color, and zilch personality. Truth be told, it felt more like purgatory than the celestial space cultivated in this cathedral! Though, I would never breathe even a hint of my displeasure to my benefactors.

People were milling about, and I felt lost in it all. Until a voice rose above the din.

"Master Grey!" a boisterous man called out from the side, with a heavy Eastern accent and from the gut.

I turned to find Archbishop Peter Kochurov lumbering toward me, a stout man with a fully, bushy dark beard streaked with silver. He was wearing the typical liturgical vestments of his tradition. White robe phelonion with gold trim, a heavy gold pectoral cross hanging around his neck and resting on his generous gut, head crowned by a beautiful red brocade mitre of crimson and gold, tipped by a complementary gold cross.

We'd had a cordial relationship the past year since I became Order Master. Met one another several times at local ecumenical functions put on by the National Cathedral, and then in North East DC at the Catholic basilica and sometimes at Georgetown when there were interesting symposia on various goings-on in religious research and archaeology. I even helped break up a fight between the archbishop and some blowhard Reformed Protestant professor over the Schism of 1054, arguing with the man over some finer point of doctrine. Didn't really take Kochurov's side, but it won me to his heart anyhow. We've been pals ever since.

I smiled warmly and extended a hand, but the man opened up for an embrace. So I obliged, the archbishop kissing both my cheeks and nearly squeezing the life out of me!

"Thank you for the invitation, Your Eminence," I said, catching my breath. "I'm only sorry I never made it down the street until now. This place is magnificent!"

"It is being smaller than that hunk of stone you call a cathedral up the road," he said in a lilting Eastern European accent, "but it is being far more beautiful, methinks!"

"I concur!"

"I am being thankful you are here to join us, but..." he looked over his shoulders. "You are alone, yes?"

I raised my brow. "Alone? Yes, my colleagues were unable to make it."

"Your, Navy SEALs for Jesus colleagues you are saying?" Kochurov said with a wry grin.

Heat ran up the back of my neck at the reference to Project SEPIO, the muscular arm of the Order of Thaddeus responsible for the more overt efforts at protecting and contending for the Christian faith. *Sepio* is Latin for 'surround with a hedge.' That's the mission of the project. To surround the memory of the faith with a hedge. To preserve and protect objects and relics of the faith, as well as the memory itself, even doctrine and matters of faith. Then there was the acronym, combining the first letters of *Sepio, Erudio, Pugno, Inviglio, Observo*. Latin for protect, instruct, fight for, watch over, heed.

The more forward-facing operations were intellectual in nature and widely known; the behind-the-scenes operations, the ones that had gotten me into trouble with the Powers-that-Be weren't.

At least, they weren't supposed to be more widely known than I thought...

Apparently there were those who were in the know.

I laughed and slapped the archbishop's back. "You've been reading too many Dan Brown novels, my friend."

The man twisted up his face and sputtered his lips as if swallowing a whole lemon. "Not that Brown fellow. I am being more inclined to reading Steve Berry. Do you know him?"

"His latest read is on my nightstand. But I must say, rumors of clandestine operations sinking the latest conspiracy to threaten the Church are greatly exaggerated."

"If you are saying so, Master Grey. At any rate, I am being most thankful you are being here this evening, especially because of your background."

"My background. Why's that?"

He shrugged. "You never know when former Army Ranger might be coming in handy."

I sensed unease in the man, so I pressed it. "Is there some sort of threat I should know about?"

"Nothing specific. But I am knowing that certain members of our Roman Catholic brothers of the faith were not being particularly happy when Pope Francis gave the delegation of the Ecumenical Patriarchate the bone fragments of Saint Peter."

"Which members? And why would they be mad?"

He waved a dismissive hand. "Nothing but rumors of some religious order seeking the purity of the Church—the *original* Church, in their minds. Some viewed Francis's gift as a capitulation to those who broke from the Mother Faith."

"I see..."

Kochurov laughed, his mouth widening into a jovial grin. "Or it is being nothing and I am reading far too many conspiracy novels of late!"

We shared a laugh, and the archbishop encouraged me to join the queue of observants waiting to get a glimpse of the relics.

I did, snaking along the outer wall toward the center until walking toward a massive wood divider adorned with more colorful icons of what looked to be apostles arrayed to the right and left of Christ seated above a narrow door leading beyond into the viewing area. It was the iconostasis, the wall of icons separating the altar portion from the rest of the nave.

Shuffling forward every few minutes after each individual act of veneration, I considered the nature of what I had previously given my life to. Relics. Those objects cherished by the Church across the spectrum—be it a piece of cloth or bone fragment or entire body—preserving the memory of a significant event or person in Christianity.

The reason I had devoted much of my professional life to studying and preserving and promoting such objects of veneration was because of the changing times. I thought they were perfect for a generation raised on the ephemeral, on the tyranny of the fleeting present, where doubt and skepticism reigned.

From my experience with the emerging generation as a professor at Princeton, people want something they can sink their teeth into, something they can experience that has tangible benefits for their lives. Unfortunately, from that same experience, it was clear that for many coming up behind me, religion doesn't offer that anymore. Which was why the ancient Christian relics were so important now, and why the Order of Thaddeus had stepped up its efforts at preserving the memory of the faith and exploiting these tangible, experiential reminders of the faith their people have forgotten and forsaken.

It's why the Shroud was so key to my research for so many years. And frankly to Nous's operation a few years ago to destroy the single greatest relic in all of Christendom: the memory of Christ's resurrection. Of course they sought to destroy it. Proving the Shroud proved Jesus' resurrection, which would have been all the Church needed to spark a new awakening belief.

Shuffling forward, I couldn't help but chuckle to myself. Boy, did that seem like a lifetime ago. Yet it'd been only three years since it all went down!

Since it all had started, the inciting incident that would unravel my professional life and thrust me into an entirely new one.

So much had changed...

And yet so much hadn't. People still longed for some sort of connection to something bigger than themselves. To make meaning out of an existence that seemed so meaningless—especially with all of life seemingly shifting into the digital, into the intangible. Perhaps reclaiming relics was just what the modern world needed to recapture the memory of faith.

Like the ones I was waiting to glimpse.

Shuffling forward again, I recalled that in the early 1940s a rather monumental discovery happened in a small niche under a monument found in the catacombs underneath Saint Peter's Basilica, dating as far back as the early second century. The discovery? The bones of Saint Peter. For safekeeping, they were stored somewhere in the Vatican and not seen again until Pope Paul VI in 1968 announced that the relic bones of Peter had been "identified in a way which we can hold to be convincing." That convincing way was the fact the remains were missing their feet.

Tradition held that the Apostle Peter had died by crucifixion. But rather than following in the footsteps of his Lord, Jesus Christ, he requested—pleaded, really—to be crucified upside down. Further, the scientific evidence showed that the remains were that of a man from the first century who died at an old age. The real kicker was that there were no feet found on the remains—no pun intended! An important detail because the Apostle not only had been crucified with his head down, but his feet were cut off afterward.

While most of those bones were interred underneath the main altar of Saint Peter's Basilica in the Vatican, nine bone fragments were placed in a bronze reliquary separate from the others. Pope Paul VI then had them placed in his private chapel in the papal apartments. There they stayed until an interesting juncture in Saint Pete's journey.

During the feast of Saints Peter and Paul in Rome on June 29, 2020, after Mass Pope Francis asked the Orthodox representatives to come with him to the papal apartments. There the pope took the reliquary placed in the chapel of his predecessor Paul VI and offered it to his guests. Delighted, they returned to Istanbul and presented them to Patriarch Bartholomew of Constantinople. At a reception and installation ceremony the next day, the patriarch said, "Pope Francis made this grand, fraternal and historic gesture and I was deeply moved. It was a brave and bold initiative of Pope Francis." It was a grand gesture in the ongoing ecumenical dialogues to repair the breach between the two wings of Christianity and bring about full communion.

Now, if only there was something that could bring Protestants into the fold, perhaps they could all sing 'Kumbaya' and call it a day, embracing one another as brothers and sisters in the same faith as Christ intended. Perhaps Martin Luther's hand, now that would bring them in!

I chuckled to myself at the funny, reaching the threshold of the wood iconostasis partition now.

My heart started picking up pace. I wiped the sweat from my palms on my pants, but it didn't seem to work. Felt as nervous as the first time I'd met Julie Lawrence's dad back in tenth grade before asking her to the high school prom! The nerves were born out of respect for the man I had always identified with. After all, it was the name I'd chosen as my confirmation name.

Peter.

Even as an early teenager, I had seen something of my story in Peter's own. A man who was prone to angry and arrogant outbursts, someone who wanted to connect to the heart of God and follow Christ to the ends of the earth, but also bore the seeds of doubt.

Of betrayal, even...

And when I reconverted, or perhaps returned back to the faith during that on-base chapel service, I felt like I had had a similar redemptive moment as Peter had on the shores of the Sea of Tiberias, when Jesus asked whether the apostle truly loved him, whether Peter was truly devoted to him—in heart, mind, and strength.

"Yes, Lord; you know that I love you..." I muttered as the door opened for me to enter, repeating Peter's declaration to Jesus.

Remarkably, Christ forgave him of his betrayal and still wanted to use him. Still wanted to build his Church upon him, the Rock, as Jesus named him. Gave me hope for my own life.

Prayed he would use me in the same way, even…

I glimpsed the sacred object of bronze gleaming through the door. Growing up I had serious reservations about venerating such objects of the faith, much to the chagrin of my thoroughly Catholic father. And when I grew in my faith later in a more Protestant variety, I thought such acts were idolatrous.

But then I had read the perspective of a famed New Testament scholar, N. T. Wright, who suggests relics can be explained in terms of God's grace working in and through the physical life of the person, even after death, their bodies becoming regarded as a special place where God's love and presence are made known, to both the faithful and those seeking faith. Figured if that Anglican could accept such practices, then so could I, which led to a rich academic career in studying such religious artifacts.

A middle-age man in a rumpled black suit exited. I took in a measured breath and stepped up to the plate.

The space behind the door was cramped. A red plush circular rug sat under a stone altar of modest proportion in the middle, with two large wood gold-cushioned chairs standing behind. Atop the altar sat a faded bronze box, the size of my old man's toolbox from childhood. The lid was thrown back, and nestled inside was a bright red puffy pillow, a chord of gold edging it.

And the bone fragments. Nine of them, white and shimmering under lights high above. Almost with a holy hue.

I caught my breath and crossed myself on instinct, stepping toward the collection of Peter's memory markers on careful feet. Heart was strumming a mean beat now, with affection more than anything, and my breaths tried keeping pace.

A shiver ran down my spine as I took in the sight of the

relics bearing the memory of the apostle's witness to the love and presence of God. A smile spread across my face at the thought of those bone fragments offering Jesus Christ himself the bread he broke at the last supper, or perhaps penning his two letters to the churches in Asia Minor that had inspired his professional life and personal faith. The bones that had been shattered during his persecution when he was crucified like his Lord, but upside down.

Taking in the sight, my heart warmed anew before the memory markers of my confirmed namesake.

And then it went cold at the sound of shots ringing through the nave.

Instinctively, I pulled out my trusty Beretta nestled at my back under my suit coat. Learned the hard way early on one of the first rules of SEPIO.

Never leave home without cold, hard steel.

Hadn't made that mistake since that fateful day in England sussing out the Holy Grail.

Glad I'd learned my lesson for such a time as this.

I spun toward the sound with outstretched hand, shielding the bronze reliquary with my back—the ominous conspiracy utterances of the archbishop sounding not so conspiratorial now.

Nothing but rumors of some religious order seeking the purity of the Church—the original Church, in their minds. Some viewed Francis's gift as a capitulation to those who broke from the Mother Faith.

Nothing but rumors, my—

More shots rang out with interruption, followed by a chorus of cries and shouts of mercy.

My view was limited by the blasted hunk of wood sandwiched between the alcove and the rest of the nave, the tiny door offering the only view. Which wasn't much.

Foreign tongues shouted now for compliance. Three, maybe four. All Italian, from the sound of it.

Not what I would have expected. Not in the slighted.

Although, if it was a faction within the Mother Faith, as Kochurov had explained, it would make sense they were Italians. Not since the first John Paul had an Italian sat on Saint Peter's throne. Albino Luciani, was his name, serving thirty-three days until his untimely death. Then a Pole succeeded him, of all people! At least, that's how many viewed it. I thought John Paul II had been a worthy successor. After all, he did bring down the Iron Curtain.

Footfalls suddenly brought me back to the moment. Coming toward my position just beyond the door. A *slap-slap-slap* against the chocolate-white marble tile I had fancied on arrival.

So I sprang into action, knowing what they were after.

Spinning back to Peter's relics, I flipped the lid close to the bronze case and snatched it with one hand, then stuffed it under my arm like a football. Three years as star quarterback with the Falls Church Jaguars had to count for something.

And what better way to put those three years to good use than protecting the First Pope's bones!

Except there was nowhere to go. Nothing but paint and gilt and stone and wood at all angles. Which weren't any to speak of since the space was shaped in a half circle.

So I did the only thing I thought to do—only thing I could do!

Hide in plain sight.

Hustling to the corner of the iconostasis that butted up against the stone building, I pivoted with my back to the polished wood.

Just as a figure wearing a brown monk's robe came rushing inside toward the altar where Saint Peter's bones had been resting. Complete with the hooded cowl and rope belt and everything.

I crouched into position, still holding the bronze box under my arm and extending my weapon toward the hostile.

Not on your life, pal...

The hostile stopped cold, muttering something to himself with wide, waving arms, head going this way and that in search of what should have been sitting on that stone altar.

But was instead cradled under my arm.

Which the hooded figure seemed to sense.

Suddenly the figure spun around toward my position.

Who turned out to be a woman. Face olive, hair dark, with onyx eyes set above high cheekbones and a crow's nose.

Didn't see that coming. Although, I'd always been an egalitarian when it came to these sorts of scenarios.

"How do you do," I said. "Don't believe we've met. And you are?"

Waiting for a reply, I adjusted my position and my grip.

On both the bronze reliquary and my trusty Beretta.

Mystery Chick didn't look armed. But who knew what she was hiding underneath that brown robe.

Like I said. An egalitarian when it comes to these sorts of scenarios.

"Who are you?" she hissed, stiffening and taking a step toward me.

"I asked you first."

Saw her jawline bulge with an irritated clench. Good. Just the way I like them. Easier to ruffle that way and keep control of the—

A chorus of screams and the shuffling of feet rose high over the wood barrier. Followed by a voice throwing some command there way.

Male, in that Mediterranean tongue again.

Nose flaring now, she thrust her hand out. "Hand it over."

"No foreplay, eh? Just straight to business?"

She took a careful step toward me now, a spark of orange

glinting off those onyx eyes of hers. Whether from some demonic possession or from the lights above, wasn't sure.

Probably the former; prayed for the latter.

But in my line of work, you prayed for the best but expected the worst.

So, demon possessed it was!

"I will be giving you," Mystery Chick said, "to the count of three to hand over the box. Or I shoot."

I smirked. Sounded like some bargain-bin Kindle thriller bad guy. Why is it always to the count of three? Why not two, why not four? Much more preferred a nice round number.

But I could see she wasn't into sarcasm.

So I said, "Sorry, lady. But you're forgetting who's armed. Now why don't you step back and get the heck—"

She shouted with interruption something in that foreign tongue I'd heard before.

A beat later, that gunfire returned.

Pop-pop.

Followed by another.

Pop-pop-pop.

Which threw up another chorus of screams and shouts of mercy.

Now she smirked, putting a hand on a set of generous hips that cinched the robe around her not-so-generous waistline.

"My men just shot two of the guests."

My men? So the she-wolf in monk's clothing was the one in charge.

And she'd just commanded them to shoot two people. Possibly dead.

Not good...

"They spared the Archbishop," Mystery Chick went on. "They won't be as merciful the next time. So hand over the box and nobody else dies."

"Except I've got you in my sights," I growled. "Literally. I can just take you as my hostage and wait out the police."

She shrugged. "Perhaps. But you're out-manned four to one. Not very good odds, methinks."

I scoffed. "For a former Army Ranger? I'll take those odds and take my chances."

Them Vegas odds, as Gapinski would say. Wished the lug was here to back me up now, because this was about to get real, real quick!

There was a shouting cry in that foreign tongue again, followed by the mystery woman's heated reply.

She outstretched her hand again and shook it. "Hand it over. *Now!* Or face the consequences."

Beretta pointed at the woman's face and eyeing the hand, I weighed the options in the span of a few seconds.

Surely the police had been notified and would be swarming the place soon.

But not soon enough to prevent the dreaded possibility of Kochurov getting shot.

And worse, dying.

But to hand over these relics of Peter...to these murderous hostiles? Unconscionable. Incomprehensible.

A desecration!

"Three seconds!" Mystery Chick shouted, snapping me back to attention.

What to do, what to do...

"One."

Hand over Peter's bone fragments or take the risk?

"Two!"

Not on Kochurov's life. Or any more after the first shots.

The woman opened her mouth for the final countdown when I stood.

Beretta still in my one hand, I opened my arm still cradling the bronze box like a football and handed over the prize.

One end of her mouth curled upward, those onyx eyes drilling me with victory.

She grabbed onto it; I drew it closer to my chest.

"This ain't over," I growled. "Not by a long shot."

She smirked, yanking the box from my arms and spinning away without a word. Hustling across the marble floor and shouting commands to her men.

I strafed across the rug with my outstretched Beretta, taking aim through the door to the iconostasis. Glimpsed three other figures clad in brown monk robes coalescing on Mystery Chick.

When one of them took aim.

At me!

Sending a *pop-pop-pop* volley of shots sailing my way.

I dove as one splintered the edge of the wood entrance. The other two sank into the stone behind.

Pretty good shot for a whack job terrorist!

I rolled and recovered pretty quickly. Banged up my shins pretty good, but nothing to write home about.

Springing back to my feet, I sprinted out into the nave, where I found chairs toppled and two bunches of groups around two downed people—one man, one woman—blood pooled underneath.

Kochurov was seated on the floor off to the side, leaning against the stone wall with a colorful icon of some apostle behind him, head lolled in a way he looked injured.

Or worse...

I ran to him, the sound of slamming doors outside catching my attention.

That would come. First things first.

"Your Eminence," I shouted, sliding into a kneel at his side. "Are you hurt?"

He lolled his head my way, opening his eyes and muttering something incoherent in his native Russian tongue. Couldn't tell if he was hurt, but there didn't seem to be any wounds on the man. Looked in shock more than anything.

The squeal of tires through the large door still standing open caught my attention outside. A large black SUV, Escalade by the look of it, sped away.

Glancing back at Kochurov, I knew I had a choice. Stay and help pick up the pieces, wait for the authorities to give a statement. Or go after Saint Peter's relic.

Wasn't really a choice, given there was nothing I could do for those who bled out, and the others could take care of themselves.

So I darted out into the night from hell, leaping down the concrete stairs and into the road.

When a car screeched to a halt, screaming at me with a blaring horn and blinding white lights.

I put my hands out to brace myself for an escape over the offending car's hood, but modern engineering being what it is, the car stopped on a dime. Black BMW. Nice ride.

And fast...

Spinning around, I caught sight of the hostiles making their escape and made another split-second decision.

Damn, I was getting tired of those things!

But I did anyway, crossing myself with my free hand and praying for the Lord's favor—right before I aimed for the Bimmer with my Beretta.

Poor guy froze stiff. Eyes going wide and wild. Hands flying up in the air in surrender.

Which was all I needed.

Hustling to the driver's side door, I gave the handle a yank. No go. Locked tight. Which made sense in these parts of town. And modern engineering being what it is, with auto lock and all.

So I shouted, "Open the door! Step out of the car!"

Same stiff freeze, same wide and wild eyes, same raised hands.

"Or I shoot!"

That did the trick.

Door opened and the man, a middle-aged Indian fellow by the look of it, murmured something in his native tongue in between sobs.

Grabbed hold of his arm and yanked him out.

"Sorry, man. I'm in a bit of a pickle and need a ride. Which at the moment is *your* ride."

"But—"

I tossed the guy to the pavement before he offered any more of a complaint. Felt bad, and there was a good chance I'd pay for this later—in more ways than one. But SEPIO was technically a sub-group of the Vatican gendarmerie and had an understanding with INTERPOL for these sorts of things. I was hoping the Feds would see it their way.

And mine.

Hoping in, I slammed the door closed and rolled down the window.

"Don't worry, I'll bring her back, safe and sound. I'm a professional at this sort of thing."

Then off I drove, the tail end of the black SUV blocks away now but quickly gaining on him.

Never was into Bimmers, but this sucker could really move! Closed the gap in no time flat, the pair of us approaching an intersection.

That flashed to yellow.

Brake lights from a sedan in front of the target slammed on its brakes—never understood those types of drivers!

And apparently the SUV didn't either, the beast flooring it and blowing into the poor civilian's backside, sending it skittering into the now-red intersection. Which threw up a whole chorus of squeals and honks and PG-13 shouts.

Not needing to damage the goods and add vandalism to my grand theft auto rap sheet, I eased the Bimmer past the poor fella and followed after the Escalade. Ironically, rounding past the National Cathedral onto Wisconsin now.

Thought about calling into the farm and eliciting Zoe Corbino's operational-support help, but knew it wouldn't matter. So I gunned it, appreciating the Germans more than I had at that point in my life. Boy, did they know how to make an engine!

My Saxon appreciation was interrupted by weapon fire.

A *rat-a-tat-tat* spray aimed at me!

I veered out of the way, escaping the brunt of it that went high and wide but definitely turned the tables.

Now things were getting real!

"I'm getting too old for this..."

But I veered back behind the whack jobs, thrusting my Beretta through the open window and taking aim.

Sending my own *pop-pop-pop* rejoinder. Then another: *pop-pop-pop.*

Shattered the read window and caught sight of some goon's head snapping forward, a geyser of dark liquid spraying around the cabin.

Didn't know who I hit; didn't care.

But his or her compadre sure did! Sent an angry, unrelenting reply with another spray of automatic rifle fire.

Rat-a-tat-tat! Rat-a-tat-tat!

Swerved this way and that, but caught it in the kisser something fierce.

Not mine; the Bimmer's. A few bullets punched wicked spiderwebby holes through the glass, another set strafed the front hood.

By the grace of the good Lord above, the Bimmer kept right on trucking.

And by the ingenuity of those German engineers, God

bless 'em!

But I couldn't let a punch like that go unchecked. So I took aim again, careful to make my shots count as we sped through the DC evening streets.

There it was. The opening. The hostile's kisser.

Which was there one minute, gone the next.

Felt bad about it and prayed for forgiveness. But I knew it was him or me.

Who knew who I hit, but with two men down I had dramatically evened the odds of survival.

And of retrieving Saint Pete's relics.

But then the SUV suddenly banked right down a side street.

Almost missed the turn, slamming the brakes and spinning the wheel to keep up. But I managed to stay on their six and floored it.

Only problem was, it was one DC's residential streets laid back before cars were a thing. So the nice wide-open plains of the Massachusetts Ave turned into a narrow nightmare, with cars lining the street on both sides dutifully parked in front of multi-million dollar row houses!

Thankfully it forced the SUV to slow down, but I had to take it easy too. Figured if I brought the Bimmer back in one piece, the owner would show me mercy, see things my way, even though there were a few scratches—

A crunching sound stage right caught my attention, my passenger's side mirror now dangling by a thread.

Or not.

I huffed a frustrated breath, trying to figure out how to end this thing.

The hostiles had to slow some more to navigate their beast through the gauntlet of cars.

Which gave me a window to act.

Reaching out, I aimed for the tires barely visible under the

SUV's backside. Even then, the blacks from the vehicle and blacktop and tires all ran together, making it hard to figure out where to shoot.

Then I saw it.

Closing an eye, I aimed for whirling tred and spat a *pop-pop-pop* volley.

Missed, missed, and missed again.

"Are you kidding me?" I cursed under my breath.

Didn't have many shots left. No way I could reload, either.

Next volley had to count.

Or it was game over.

So I took in a stabilizing breath, lined up the shot again, then sent a single shot sailing into its left wheel.

Connection!

Sending the SUV limping on its back leg.

And rubber slapping against the pavement and flapping pieces flying and sparks flaring up.

Right before it hit a pothole that sent the beast spinning to one side.

And then banging into one of the moored cars.

The force of it all sent the beast mounting the row of parked cars until it slid back down to the street and toppled onto its back.

Better her than me! But then there was the matter of Peter's relics.

Perhaps it should have been me instead!

Throwing the Bimmer into 'Park,' I slid out and ran to the overturned car.

There was shattered glass everywhere, blue ice strewn across the street like a polar vortex had blown our way. The smell of gasoline was strong, as well as blotches of green antifreeze and black oil streaking my path. The engine hissed on my approach, like a wounded animal that was ready to bite back.

A bite that could be an inferno if I didn't hop to it.

Which would sort of defeat the point of the car chase in the first place!

Holding my Beretta steady, I ran over to the backside of the overturned beast. I could see the two bodies I'd shot earlier inside the rear seat.

Both male, both dead.

Padding around toward the driver, and getting a strong whiff of gas now, I saw his head lolling outside the window, blood running from his mouth to the street beneath.

That meant three down. Only one to go.

But as I squeezed past the fender mercilessly close to some silver European sedan, I rounded the front to find something peculiar.

Where I expected to find the fourth person, Mystery Chick by my count, the passenger's side was empty. Windshield was shattered and door closed. Must have been ejected during the crash.

A small bit of irony for you. The woman who crashed our relic veneration party was crashed herself.

Kept my Beretta steady anyhow. Learned early that no amount of irony can replace the possibility of funny business rearing its ugly head.

Padded along the front with the passenger's compartment in view. Door was closed. Inside, I could see what I had come for. The fruits of all this car-chasing labor.

Saint Peter's relics.

I shoved my Beretta at my back and went to open the door.

But it was locked tight. Or jammed shut, given the topsy-turvy adventure it just had.

I worked at it some more, but it was no use. I looked inside the door window and there it was. Peter's reliquary just lying there on the ceiling, and just out of reef!

Glancing around, I took off my suit coat and withdrew my

weapon again. Then I wrapped the jacket around the Beretta and whacked at the window.

One. Two. Three. Four!

It finally shattered.

I put the Beretta at my back again and used the coat to clear away the glass. Then reached inside and opened the door.

Easy peasy!

I reached in and grabbed the box, the lid still securely closed.

When I withdrew from the cabin, I saw something run out of the shadows from the corner of my eye.

Dark, lithe, and readying for an attack.

Didn't have time enough to react, but I did bend and throw my arms up to soak up the blow.

Contact!

The box tumbled from my hand to the hard pavement below.

So did I, the kick a powerful one against my raised arms, sending me down hard.

Box went one way; I went another.

Thankfully it didn't open—but that'll leave a mark.

Scrambling up from the pavement, I brought my arms up just as another blow came my way. Then another.

Fortunate for me, I was president of the Tae Kwon Do Club at Georgetown my senior year. So I knew a thing or two about this sort of thing.

Blocked each blow with ease, focusing on defense since I was caught off guard and the perp was quick on the one-two punch draw.

Until another one slipped through and connected with my jaw.

I grabbed it, turning it this way and that while hopping back a few paces on the balls of my feet.

And then saw it. The street light catching the perp just right.

Mystery Chick!

Lost the monk's get up, exchanging it for some tight-fitting black one instead. Face was flecked with blood, and she had a nasty gash on the side of her head. The rolling crash did a number on her, alright.

But clearly not good enough.

"You again," she growled, hips swinging into position and arms raising to bring it again.

"I was brought up to never hit a girl," I said, breathless and aching from the blow. "But in your case, I think I'll make an exception."

She screamed and came at me. And I meant what I said.

Readied my hands to strike first and faked right—which sent Mystery Chick ducking—but hooking left instead.

Catching her square in the jaw.

She sailed backward, landing hard on her back. She lay still.

I winced from the blow, shaking out the ache in my hand, and sauntered over.

Mystery Chick lay still and sprawled, out cold. Head one way, legs another, arms out and about.

But on my approach, the closer I got, something didn't look right.

Then I saw it. Arm bent with her hand underneath at her back.

It all happened in slo-mo after that.

Put it together just as that arm started withdrawing.

Sending me reaching for my Beretta stuffed at my own back.

Just as some Heckler & Koch barrel came sliding out from under Mystery Chick and aiming my way.

More German engineering!

But not before I had already withdrawn my Italian-engineered pistol.

And popped off four shots before she knew what was what.

One sank into the pavement above her head. Another hit her right shoulder. The other two sank into her chest.

It was over. Just like that.

Mystery Chick slumped into the road, her arm falling hard and the H&K resting in her limp hand.

I shuffled to it and kicked it aside, then bent down to the woman.

Her chest was seeping dark crimson now, and her face was expecting the inevitable. Eyes wide, mouth searching for breath.

Had to get to the bottom of this before it was lights out for her.

"Who are you, really?" I asked, taking the woman's face in my hand and directing it toward mine.

Her mouth gasped for a breath before she gave her answer: "I'm nobody,"

"Who do you work for?"

"Myself," she whispered.

"There's rumor you're part of an underground Catholic order seeking to purify the Church. Is that right?"

Now she smiled, a giggle slipping through.

"No Order. Pirate."

"Pirate?" I asked, not understanding.

She swallowed, gasping for air now.

"No, no, no..." I shook her face. "Stay with me. Why do you say pirate?"

"Lots of money in relics." Another grasp for breath. "Especially *Svyatoy Petr...*"

Didn't take a genius to know she was talking about Peter's relics. But now she was speaking Russian, which was confusing.

"So it was about money?"

I caught a nod, her eyes closing now and face draining of color.

Couldn't help but chuckle at the thought of it all.

So no grand conspiracy. Nothing religious about it. Unless you take Jesus' teachings on the Sermon on the Mount seriously, that you can't serve both God and Mammon.

God or money.

Sirens were blaring now. Last I needed was to get entangled in something on this scale, not with the Order's board of directors breathing down my neck.

So I grabbed the bronze box of Peter's relics and slid back into the Bimmer, figuring the owner would want his ride back.

Then I made the trek back to the cathedral, glad that for once there was no vast conspiracy to contend with, or another kid on the conspiratorial block giving me more paperwork.

Money. Makes the world go round, I guess.

Sliding through a yellow light, I chuckled to myself.

Sometimes people's motivations really are that simple.

STORY 2
GILDED BONES

The sign read "Celestial Bjorn," and I knew I was in for a world of hurt.

It was held by a stocky man with a comb for a mustache and a comb over for a haircut, wearing an ill-fitting black suit and rumply white shirt and slim black tie—clearly trying a bit hard with the attire. The gent was leaning against a post and slurping a Starbucks at the baggage claim.

I cringed inside and groaned. Just my luck.

After the all-night flight from Dulles International Airport, I wished I had rented my own vehicle for the drive over. But Zoe Corbino, my trusty operational support director, had arranged a pickup after the lengthy flight. She wanted me to be able to focus on the coming task rather than worrying about navigating my way to the mission target. She was probably right, but I was not fancying this trip. Not in the slightest.

But I strolled up to the bloke anyway and introduced myself.

"No, I'm here for the lady on the sign," he said with a dismissive slurp of his Starbucks. Coffee, too, which made it all the worst.

I cleared my throat and smiled flatly. "I *am* the lady on the sign. Celeste Bourne. Not Celestial Bjorn."

He furrowed his brow and looked at the sign, trying to make out what had happened. What happened was he smoked a few too many spliffs before coming to pick me up, that's what!

Silas, I'm going to kill you...

"With the Vatican," I added, hoping that flashing those credentials would put two and two together.

That seemed to register something in the inner recesses of the man's strung-out brain. He glanced at the sign, then at me. "Are you sure you're not Celestial Bjorn?"

"Don't I wish..." I muttered. Strolling toward the receiving line outside the terminal, I shouted, "Well, come along. My chariot awaits, I presume?"

There was a shuffling of feet from behind and a "Yes, ma'am" in that horrid guttural dialect of the Netherlands I so loathed. A right nutter, he was.

Rain was coming down in angry sheets outside, the terminal a perfect cliché for the nation who made a name for itself reclaiming the land from such cantankerous bouts of nature. Rumpled Man hurried past and guided me to an awaiting chariot parked in the taxicab lane with its flashers on.

I groaned at the sight, but followed anyway.

It was a sad sort of hackney. Nothing like the regal black carriages for hire running about through my homeland, England. Just a silver Mercedes without even the comforts of leather! Climbing inside with my carry on, the cabin reeked of boiled cabbage and meatballs, reminding me why I always drove myself, even on mission.

Especially on mission!

The cabby slid inside and started the car, then jolted from the curb on toward our rendezvous point.

The Hague.

More specifically, the Hague Penitentiary Institution.

Silas had rung me the day before yesterday using that voice of his he reserves for the special occasion he wants something. Usually a right good snogging in the back seat of his Jeep Wrangler, but quite often something special for the Order of Thaddeus. Our mutual employer.

I'm usually one to oblige. Especially the snogging in the back of his Jeep Wrangler, given we are engaged to be married. Although I'd much prefer something European made to the American iconic vehicle. But it's something about teenage nostalgia, or something or other that made him spring for the car.

At any rate, he really ginned up the fiancé charm this time, insisting he would handle it himself but was loaded down with paperwork, reminding me for the umpteenth time that the job of Order Master is one tireless, never-ending stream of administrative nonsense. And I reminded him it wouldn't be if he would hire an executive assistant, as we've all been badgering him for the better part of a year. Administration was definitely not his strong suit.

Torres was still on that archaeological dig of hers and Gapinski was the last person SEPIO wanted interviewing a thief tried by the international courts for cultural crimes against humanity. So I was left holding the bag.

And quite a bag it was.

I had flown a third of the way across the world to interrogate an Albanian man who had been brought up on charges in the International Criminal Court for stealing the relic arm of Saint Polycarp of Smyrna from the Holy Monastery of the Dormition of the Theotokos in Ambelakiotissa in the mountainous Nafpaktos of Greece.

The early Church martyr had been the bishop of the Roman Smyrnean province and died a gruesome death at the hands of the empire for refusing to renounce his faith in Jesus Christ. He had been venerated by the Church ever since, his remains serving as a memory marker for his wholehearted, faithful commitment to his faith in Christ.

The relic had gone missing March 2013, seemingly vanishing from its proper place of veneration. It was quite the scandal in the ecclesiastical community, a relic of such import being stolen as such, not to mention amongst the Greeks. The government spared no expense to right the wrong, employing its investigative forces to bring about a resolution. When they did, they caught a break.

Poor bloke who burgled the relic wasn't too keen of a burglar, the man having left fingerprints and genetic material of the sacrilegious offender. He also left behind a trail of incriminating communicative evidence in digital form. Messages and telephone calls from his cellphone on the night of the theft had arisen in the same area of the theft, which were discovered after warrants were issued.

For much of 2013, recovering the right hand of Saint Polycarp was a high priority for the police, as there was a keen interest in recovering the artifact in ecclesiastical circles and it was a considerable blow to the national ego. Senior officers of the Greek Police were in constant communication with Metropolitan Hierotheos of Nafpaktos for much of the year throughout the course of the investigation, joined by INTERPOL in an effort to recover the cultural icon.

The Albanian man was apprehended trying to cross the northern border back to his homeland. However, the relic wasn't on his person, and he was tight-lipped as to its whereabouts. He, however, was promptly handed over to international authorities and tried for his crimes. The relic has remained missing the past eight years, never to be seen from again.

Which is where my little jaunt to the Hague came in.

The Albanian was nearing the end of life. Terminal pancreatic cancer. So when the chap passed, so did the location of the lost relic. The case had languished with INTERPOL over the last several years, and along the way SEPIO got dragged into the affair. It also ended up into some X-file in a drawer in HQ.

Until Silas Grey got hold of it.

Silas being Silas, he became intrigued about the missing artifact, wondering why it hadn't been recovered after all these years. His interest in the early Church, especially early martyrs, compounded by the inner relicologist—needless to say the Order Master couldn't let the case go. But rather than closing the bloody case himself, he got his fiancé to do it for him.

Me.

Hence the trip through the Dutch countryside getting pummeled by a thunderstorm on toward destiny in a hackney that smelled more like a West Sussex pub!

"We're here, missy," the driver said, followed by a rumble of thunder in the distance, as if putting an exclamation point on the announcement.

Dark clouds hung ominously above the penitentiary, the face of which was simply ghastly. All brick, no personality. Which is to say, very Dutch. Two oversized turrets trying too hard stood guard with a broad wooden gate at the middle, closed and unwelcoming.

The cabbie pulled in front of the massive doors. A poor chap with a deep scowl sauntered out into the unrelenting rain underneath a pitiful black umbrella that wouldn't have done anyone any good.

After flashing my credentials at the guard and explaining my business, we were ushered through the gate. The hackney carted me into an inner courtyard and dropped me off at an entrance. After exchanging the fare, I bid him adieu and off he went, as well as I.

Credentialing myself once more at a voice box, I was buzzed inside and I ushered myself into a rather austere, utilitarian vestibule manned by a gent at a metal desk. He looked up from a magazine on my arrival, then stood.

"Celeste Bourne," I said on approach, pulling out my SEPIO ID card. "Here to administer an interrogatory interview of prisoner 62352791."

The man, short and rather moleish by my estimation, eyed a computer monitor and nodded. He picked up a receiver, and within a few minutes a tall blonde who put an exclamation point on the Dutch height advantage appeared through a door behind the moleish attendant.

"Right this way, Ms. Bourne," she said without a smile.

I was led down a long corridor built of the same personalityless brick from outside, painted institutional white this time. Soon we arrived at a door with a black security panel. She flashed her card against it, and opened the door upon an audible click.

Another corridor greeted us. The hallway was lined by doors painted robin's egg blue, with tiny windows bared by mesh wire. Security pads anchored the handles, which told me they were jail cells. The air was tepid, humid, cloying and clawing at me. As if those inside, whoever they were, were reaching through their gates to drag me into their eternal hell.

Whilst working for the Crown's government, I had been to some remarkable prisons in the crotches of the world, chief amongst them Pakistan and Afghanistan—once as a prisoner myself. But knowing the worst international criminals, genocidal generals and ne'er-do-well dictators, were behind those doors sent a shiver creeping up my spine, and sent me scurrying to keep up.

Increasing my pace at the thought, the lady led me through another door after administering the same security protocol. Beyond was a modest room of eight or so cubicles with low barriers arrayed around a central table. In the middle, a man and two others were in conversation.

We made for them. As we drew near, the voice sounded oddly familiar.

Nearing, there was a tone and timbre to it that struck me as eerily so. A flash from another lifetime ago, back when I still pined for Her Majesty's international intelligence service.

Was that—No! It couldn't be...

I took a careful step forward and leaned to the side, craning for a better view—heat rising up the back of my neck and flushing my cheeks with recognition at the lanky, lithe man bent over the center table, with those broad shoulders and sleeves rolled up revealing the tattoo I witnessed being applied one late night. Arabic for *Destiny*.

"Nicky McGrath?" I said with an incredulous gasp, entering the cubicle space.

The chap turned around and literally dropped his jaw, and almost dropped his folder of papers he was carrying, before his mouth widened into the grin I fell for all those years ago.

"Celeste *Bourne*?" He took a hesitant step, as if disbelieving those emerald eyes of his set above those angular cheekbones. "*The* Bourne before that bloody Bourne fellow was an international Bourne sensation?"

That heat returned, and I returned a giggle. "The one and only..."

He leaned in, sort of, as did I until we chuckled with nervous energy at the gaff and just leaned in for a professional embrace. Which was very different from the last time I'd leaned into Nicholas McGrath.

Ex-colleague with MI6 and ex-boyfriend for a brief spell. Nothing dodgy, nothing intimate; had decided long ago that department was reserved for future Mr. Bourne. But enough to send my head whirling.

Except I had no time for teenage antics. Time to put on the big-girl pants and get to it.

So I swallowed and prayed the Lord would promptly whisk me away.

It didn't work.

"Nicky, I didn't know you were part of this investigation." I slapped on a smile, but my voice quivered with a revealing nervous energy.

"And I had no idea *you* were the mystery agent on loan to us from across the pond. Something about a secret society buried in the bowels of the Vatican?"

"Actually, an ecumenical Christian Order buried in the bowels of the Washington National Cathedral."

"Same difference."

"I see the decade has left you as religiously barbaric as the last time I left you."

Now he laughed. "'Tis true. Part of the growing spiritual-but-not-religious crowd."

"But are you now employed by the Hellenic Police?"

"Goodness no! Still with MI6 but on loan to INTERPOL and their cultural crime's division. After your boss, a one Mr. Grey, got in touch with us. And by getting in touch, I mean browbeat us into finally submitting to his demands."

"That's Silas for you," I said with a bit too much familiarity.

Which Nicky promptly picked up on.

He grinned and crossed his arms. "Really? Do tell…"

I frowned. "Let's keep this about the case, shall we?"

"You're no fun."

"Good chap."

"Anyway, I was brought in to supervise the interview. And jolly well glad I was, considering…"

I laughed, but moved on. Ever the flirt. "So who is our thief, anyhow?"

Nicky handed me a thick file. "Name is Jozif Brahimi."

I considered this, flipping through the stack of papers.

"Joseph Abraham. Interesting. Do we know anything more about him?"

"Male. Mid-forties. Brown eyes, brown hair. A rather ghastly sixty kilos after contracting pancreatic cancer. Likes long walks on the beach and even longer nights in bed."

I frowned, handing back the file. "Pancreatic cancer, eh?"

He tossed it to the table. "That's right. Not many more months to live, so I suppose your boss was fortunate to catch him when he did."

"The Lord works in mysterious ways."

"None of that Jesus stuff with me, please," Nicky said with the smirk I adored back in the day. Now, not so much. "I'm certifiably a None."

"Duly noted."

He went on, "Jozif was part of a radical Islamic movement in Algeria, part of the Salafi splinter movement of Sunni Islam."

"Of course," I smirked. "Aren't they all?"

Now Nicky scoffed. "Ever the xenophobe."

"Am not! Just stating the bald face of it, given our experiences the last decade."

"I suppose so, but it doesn't appear his radicalism had anything to do with the actual theft."

"Really?"

"Apparently it was all about the money."

"Aren't they all?"

"Shall we get to it, then?" He retrieved the thick file from the table and gestured toward a door at the back of the room.

I followed his gesture, a dark void anchored at one end with a tiny glass window alighted yellow.

"What, now?"

"I do suppose we could go get manicures beforehand. Perhaps waltz down to the closest High Street looking for sundresses to wear at our evening soiree."

I threw him a look that told him to back off; he did.

My blood pressure suddenly spiked, a queasiness suddenly overcoming me along with a light-headedness that compounded my embarrassment. Hadn't expected to share the interview with someone else, much less a former colleague. And former love.

But the stiff upper lip is what us Brits were bread to showcase. So showcase I did.

"Let's get to it then."

I led the way, reaching the door and fumbling with the knob.

Locked.

"Allow me," Nicky said, poking a key in the lock and letting us inside.

It was bright yellow. Far brighter than I would have liked it, or chosen as a backdrop for the interrogation. But that was Nicky for you. A by-the-books sort of lad who would crank the light to the max to throw off the interrogatee. I much more preferred low lighting. Lulled the target into a sense of ease and familiarity. Less stress tended to lend better results, the tongue loosening as the mind relaxed. Apparently Her Majesty's government had other ideas, as well as Nicky and INTERPOL.

At the center of the concrete room, painted the same utilitarian white as the rest of the building, was a metal table stood bolted to the floor. No other windows or tables. Seated at it was the suspect.

Reminded me of the late Steve Jobs, who similarly passed from pancreatic cancer. Rail thin, the orange prison jumper wilting from his frail frame, his face like a hot wax figure, the skin dripping off the bones and waiting for a last repose. His dark hair was long and stringy, but his eyes were surprisingly bright and affecting, following me as I came in after Nicky.

Jozif was chained to his chair, which was anchored to the floor. Two chairs awaited us. Nicky pulled one out for me; I sat.

He didn't take the other, preferring to stand and lean against its back.

So that's how it's going to be. Good cop, bad cop.

Who was whom—only time would tell.

Nicky stepped up to the plate first, setting the file on the table with a thud.

"Jozif Brahimi, I am special investigator Nicholas McGrath with INTERPOL." He gestured to me, continuing, "And this is Celeste Bourne with...well, an intermediary serving at the pleasure of INTERPOL."

I tried not to frown, but after that inauspicious introduction, how could I not?

"Do you know why we are here?"

The man didn't stir. Didn't even blink or part his closed mouth. I wondered if the chap was even breathing, he was so statue still.

"Jozif, you have been tried and found guilty of stealing a valuable cultural icon of the Hellenic Republic, sentenced to life in prison. We want to give you the chance to set things right."

Again, nothing.

Now Nicky crossed his arms with a sigh, leaning back to make himself tall. Imposing. In control.

Just like the man I remembered way back when.

He continued litigating the case, going over the finer points of what was known about the heist.

I half listened, but my mind also drifted to the fact of the matter.

That I was sitting in some interrogation cell in the Netherlands trying to locate a long-lost relic.

I crossed a leg at the thought, keeping my eyes trained on the man whilst considering what it was I was after.

Relics had never been part of my religious upbringing. Was far too institutional for my parents' liking, who much more preferred their Christianity freelance. While I grew up in the Church, I didn't grow up in *a* church, and anything that smacked of institutionalism was roundly rejected by Mummy and Daddy. Then, when I eventually embraced Christ as my own Lord and Savior, I had reservations about venerating such objects of the faith, believing such acts were idolatrous.

Which was a bit ironic now. Because not only was I readying to extract the location of a rather obscure, yet important, relic from a thief, I was engaged to be married to one of the primer relicologists in the world.

One end of my mouth curled upward at the thought whilst Nicky continued on with his litigation, recalling how Silas and I first became acquainted: through his work on the Shroud of Turin, the Christian relic of all Christian relics! Which eventually led me to partnering with him on several more missions, and him becoming my boss, and then his fiance.

What a whirlwind the past few years had been!

But back to the task at hand. Relics.

In graduate school, I grew in my appreciation for these memory markers of the faith. A Brit eventually won me over: the New Testament scholar, N. T. Wright suggests relics can be explained in terms of God's grace working in and through the physical life of the person, even after death, their bodies becoming regarded as a special place where God's love and presence are made known, to both the faithful and those seeking faith. Figured if the Bishop of Durham could accept such practices, then I could as well.

Not that I fancied myself a relic venerator or anything. Not in the academic sense, as Silas had; not in the religious sense as others had. It was an appreciation from afar, though I understood the value of retaining these touch points to our collective Christian past. And this one was of particular note.

Polycarp, Bishop of Smyrna, who had been cancelled before canceling was in cultural vogue.

His death was a captivating account of his uncompromising adherence to the vintage Christian faith in the face of a militantly anti-Christian culture. The Church of Smyrna wrote about this account to a neighboring church as an encouragement during times of intense apostasy and persecution by antichrists in their day. Perhaps that was precisely why such a touch point was valuable in our day, given the rising sense of cancelation in the West for beliefs that run against the progressive grain.

And it seemed time to remind the good thief of that point.

Nicky took a breath after his opening statement, offering a window for me to act.

"I wonder if I could interject," I said, holding up a finger.

"By all means, Agent Bourne."

Had to smile at that. Agent Bourne. Hadn't been an agent, in the traditional MI6 sense, in over a decade. Somehow it brought me back to it all. To us, even.

I cleared my throat and got on with it. "Jozif—may I call you that?"

Of course, I knew I could. But it was a disarming tactic I had used back in the field. A way for the interrogatee to grant me permission. I found the more they engaged in such openness, the more they opened up. I hoped it worked here.

He starred at me flatly through hollow, blank eyes. The man's sallow skin looked more dreadful now under the fluorescent lights, almost translucent, which added a measure of haunting dread to the man I was about to interrogate.

A few beats ticked by, but he nodded.

"Good. Well, then, Jozif. As Nicky—or rather, Agent McGrath indicated, my name is Celeste Bourne. I am an agent with SEPIO, an outfit with a Christian religious order called the Order of Thaddeus. We seek to promote Christianity through various projects, one of which is the recovery, preservation, study, and sharing of Christian relics. Hence, why I travelled across the world to have a bit of a chat with you."

Again, those hollow eyes, sunk behind sickly cheekbones, starred at me without emotion, without indication of anything. Should be interesting.

"As you know, what brings me here today is the matter of Saint Polycarp—patron saint of earaches, actually, which I sort of find amusing."

A sudden flinch in those eyes set me back on my feet. A glance to the left before shifting right, indicating the man was hiding both truths and lies. Wasn't expecting a tell so soon. This *was* getting interesting.

"At any rate, there is an account of his martyrdom, aptly titled *The Epistle Concerning the Martyrdom of Polycarp*, which primarily depicts him as a sort of kindly, saintly old man. However, he was also a fierce guardian of orthodoxy. Told the heretic Marcion that he was *'the first-born of Satan'* to his face, he did, for denying that the Old Testament is Scripture. One of the reasons the Order is so keen to recover his memory marker, given recent assaults upon vintage Christianity."

"Sounds like quite the character," Jozif finally said, voice high and heady. And also surprisingly strong. There was a hoarseness to it, but with real air behind it.

Which was heartening, to be sure, to find him engaging so soon.

I propped my elbows on the table, then my chin on my hands and smiled. "Are you a religious man, Jozif?"

He shrugged. "I suppose so."

Nicky scoffed from behind. "Suppose so? You are a known member of the Salafi splinter movement of Sunni Islam, with known associates confirming as much."

At this Jozif shifted, his manacles echoing loudly in the room. He frowned, but nodded. "Fine. What of it?"

"As a religious man," I went on, seizing control again, "I

assume you understand the affinity we humans have toward sacred objects. Such as Muhammed's battle standard, even his hair and tooth. Suppose an American were to abscond with those sacred relics of your holy prophet."

He leapt in his seat, the whole room seeming to shake now as he bared his teeth at me and bugged his eyes like a maniac whilst screaming something in Albania, then in Arabic. Would have leapt right over the table and tried to strangle me had he not been restrained!

Nearly leapt back myself, but I managed to remain seated.

Nicky shouted at him to calm himself, and two guards appeared, rushing over to restrain him and command calm.

For my part, I remanded in my chair, though took a bit of a breath to wind down my heart. Thankful for those years with MI6 to hone my nerves into the steel they are, flinching a bit but otherwise not giving the man the satisfaction.

Or the power.

Finally the man calmed himself, appearing as if the wind had gotten knocked out of him. Imagined he used up every last morsel of energy to come at me. Hopefully it would be his last, and the energy drain would tilt in my favor.

I straightened my jacket and crossed a leg, grabbing his file on the table. "Now, where were we? I did not mean to offend, Jozif. I was merely trying to explain what it might feel like for Christians to have a similar relic absconded with."

"I have maintained my innocence from the beginning!" he bellowed.

"Stuff and nonsense is what that is," Nicky said as I flipped through the file. "The evidence is incontrovertible, and you were declared guilty by a unanimous verdict. And don't forget the fact you confessed, you bloody scammer!"

"That was coerced!"

"Oh, bloody hell it was not!"

Jozif and Nicky went back and forth whilst I had a flip

through the file. Covered all the relevant evidential reports. The surveilling of his mobile device, the first interrogations in which the man did at first confess. Then there was his past work, which was minimal and substandard for his age; his association with Salafism, along with the radical plots that had been uncovered by particular cells in his hometown; his known associates, including friends, an old girlfriend, and mum, but no father.

I studied that portion some more as the two men continued going at it.

Something was in this folder that hadn't yet been considered. Something that would break the case open, I just knew it. Something niggling, something nagging at me to pay attention.

But what?

Setting the folder down, I stood and pulled out my mobile, walking to the exit.

"Celeste?" Nicky called out.

I put up a hand and left, calling HQ for a check-in.

And for some assistance.

"Hey, Celeste," Zoe answered, the clattering of a keyboard coming through. "How goes it?"

"Well, I've made it to the Hague and have just stepped out for some air, and some help."

"Sure thing."

"Zoe, first of all..." I turned away from the guards standing at the ready and whispered into my mobile, "why did no one tell me about Nicky McGrath?"

"Who's Nicky McGrath?"

"My ex-partner at MI6 and ex-boyfriend!"

"Oof. That's not at all awkward. Is he hot?"

"What?" I exclaimed, Nicky turning toward me and heat rising to my cheeks. I smiled and waved him away, then left. I hissed a reply, "No, he isn't hot. Well, he is a bit lush—that isn't the point!"

Zoe returned to her clattering. "Mmm-hmm. Does Silas know you're spending the day with your former lover?"

"Apparently not, if he stuck me with the chap all day. And don't call him my former lover. Sounds super dodgy that way. Anyway, I need a favor."

"Something lover-boy can't fix?"

"Zoe..."

She cleared her throat. "Sorry. Shoot."

"We're looking into the theft of the Saint Polycarp relic."

"Right. The gilded appendage."

"Hand, yes. The suspect, who was convicted, is named Jozif Brahimi. To say he has been less than cooperative is an understatement, but my gut tells me the bloke knows where the relic ended up."

"And what do you want me to do about it?"

"Look into his background, his known associates, particularly his family."

"What specifically do you want me to delve into?"

"Everything. Bank records, financials, international travel, medical records, criminal records, real estate transactions—anything that might shed light on the situation, including his family."

"What kind of light?"

I paused, considering the question. "Not sure. But I'll know it when I see it."

Zoe said she'd get on it and asked if I'd fetch Nicky's number for her. I told her to bugger off and promptly ended the call. Then reentered the interrogation room.

Meeting me at the door, Nicky asked, "Everything alright?"

"Perfectly. Why?"

"Just making sure you weren't getting cold feet. That you weren't getting scared off with Jozif putting your feet to the fire." He smiled and winked.

"Which is it? Cold or hot feet?"

He furrowed his brow without answer.

"I think you're mixing metaphors there, Nicky." I patted him on the arm and retook my seat, ready to reengage—and retake the conversation.

"May I tell you his story, Polycarp's?" I asked, again with the permission getting.

He blinked, then nodded.

So I went for it. "His martyr's story begins amidst a violent persecution of the Smyrnean church. His friends begged him to leave the region, but he refused. Instead of fleeing, he remained stubbornly, faithfully fixed inside a country house not far from the city and praying for the Church. Soon, the Empire came for the bishop after torturing a houseboy to learn of the man's whereabouts. When they arrived, the old man came downstairs and ordered that his captors be given food and drink. All he asked in return was for an hour of prayer to prepare for his prophesied demise. He ended up praying out loud for two hours and all were struck with awe and regret. Finally, the bishop was placed atop a donkey and marched into the city, where he was persuaded to renounce his faith. *'Come now,'* some men pleaded, *'where is the harm in just saying* Caesar is Lord, *and offering the incense, and so forth, when it will save your life?'*"

Jozif's head cocked to the side. He grunted, "What is that about?"

"The imperial cult of emperor worship," I explained. "'Twas a central component of life in the Empire, and one that became grounds for the imperial pogrom of Christian persecution when believers refused to worship Caesar as Lord, instead insisting that Jesus is Lord and worshiping only him as such."

Shifting in my chair and drawing closer to the man, I continued, "At any rate, their pleas for him to worship the Emperor fell on deaf ears, and eventually Polycarp was led into the town arena. There, a deafening cry for his blood arose. He was brought before the governor, who also urged Polycarp to recant. But Polycarp would not relent. Instead, he strode toward his death with head held high, then fell silent. A silence that felt like an eternity, never dipping his head and never averting his gaze from his condemner."

"Sounds like an honorable man."

Interesting revelation, to hear the interrogatee finding favor with the object of his thievery. I tucked it in my head and moved on.

I nodded. "He was. Finally, Polycarp addressed the ruler: *'Eighty and six years have I served him, acting as the servant of this Christ you yourself revile, and he never did me any injury, he has done me no wrong. Answer me this: How then can I blaspheme my King, the one who saved me?'*"

There was a sigh from behind, and a shuffling of the feet.

Was Nicky exasperated with my interrogation?

I glanced behind to find the man standing tall, with arms crossed and a cross-looking face.

Throwing him a furrowed-brow, frowning look of irritation, I went back to my story.

My interrogation!

"To which the crowd responded with thunderous, resounding mockery, casting vegetables at him from the stands. The proconsul threatened him with death by lion mauling, and Polycarp said to call them! The Roman official threatened him with fire consumption, and he bellowed for him to bring it on! So the emperor did, but also by the bishop's willing hands—who placed them behind himself for the guards to bind, giving not a struggle when they secured him. Like a distinguished ram taken out of a great flock for sacrifice and prepared to be an acceptable burnt-offering unto God."

I took a pause, letting the words settle. Jozif swallowed, never taking his eyes off from me.

"Miraculously," I continued, "something curious happened:

The fire seemed to shape itself into the form of an arch, like the sail of a ship when filled with the wind. Instead of consuming Polycarp, it circled the body of the martyr! It was reported that Polycarp appeared within the flames not like flesh which is burnt, but as bread that is baked, or as gold and silver glowing in a furnace. And it was perceived that such a sweet odor had come from the pyre, as if frankincense or some such precious spices had been smoking there.

"The ruler motioned the guards toward the fire, issuing a command to pierce Polycarp through with a dagger. And one did, striking his stomach and slashing his neck. Soon, the flames hissed to nothing, having been dowsed by the martyr's blood. The guards then built a new pyre and set it ablaze, eventually casting Polycarp's body upon it, where it was instantly consumed. Eventually, Christians laid hold of his remains, and the Church has been venerating him ever since."

"What does any of this have to do with me?" Jozif finally spoke again.

"Not so much you as it does your mum."

He stiffened, eyes briefly going wide and chest rising suddenly with a startled breath. More tells that told me I was on to something I had seen earlier in his file.

Now he narrowed his eyes and swallowed. "What about my mother?"

"She's a devout Christian, is she not?"

No answer. But like any good attorney, I already knew it.

"Greek Orthodox, actually, isn't that right?"

Now he shifted, but again remained mum.

"Baptized into the Church, raised and confirmed. Daddy passed, but Mum was a faithful Christian who even faithfully brought you up in the same faith, isn't that right?"

He lunged for me again with a scream: "*WHAT DOES ANY OF THIS HAVE TO DO WITH ME?!*"

A hot, stale, vinegary breath washed over me as the guards

rushed into the room. I was more steeled this time around, so it wasn't a surprise. But the stench turned my stomach.

As they got him under control again, my mobile rang.

I pulled it out. Zoe.

Right on cue.

"Yes, Zoe. Tell me you have something."

She explained what she had found, the maniac carrying on with surprising strength.

Slowly, a victorious grin spread across my face.

I knew exactly where the relic was hiding all these years.

"Thanks, Zoe. You're a champ!"

Stuffing the phone in my pocket, I returned to my seat.

Nicky whispered in my ear. "What's going on, mate?"

I waved him off and plowed forward.

"Your mother has a record in immigration control of making a visit across the Hellenic border."

Jozif's eyes fell, but he stirred not, saying nothing.

"The day before you were arrested."

More nothing, which wasn't surprising.

"I've also learned of an unfortunate ailment your mother has suffered."

I could sense Nicky perking up, leaning toward Jozif with interest.

Who remained still, as if dying now from the weight of realizing what was coming.

"A dreadfully difficult ear condition that makes it almost unbearable to live, with all that ringing and aching, like a bee burrowed deep in her skull."

More stillness.

"It was a throwaway comment earlier, but it's true: Polycarp is the patron saint of earaches. Did you know that, Jozif?"

He stirred now, shifting and wincing. Sweating, even, a line of perspiration beading at his hairline.

I leaned forward now, going for the kill. "Or did she know?

Did she put you up to it, knowing that the very cure that would relieve her misery was sitting in an Orthodox church across the border?"

Jozif gasped, eyes going wide and mouth hanging open. Which was all I needed.

I looked to Nicky, one end of my mouth curling upward with satisfaction. I still had it. After all these years.

"Right, jolly good," Nicky said. "I think we've got all we need now."

I stood. "Agreed."

The two of us went to leave, clearly having all we needed by the look of it.

"No, wait..." Jozif said weakly, trying to rise for a renewed fight but knowing the jig was up.

I turned back, finding a defeated, broken man. A man who knew his mum was in the dock.

"It wasn't her fault!" he said, sobbing now, with head buried in his chest. "It wasn't her fault!"

I smiled. "I know, Jozif. But we'll be needing that relic anyhow."

I was right, of course. INTERPOL in coordination with EU authorities and the help of MI6's direction under Nicky's leadership recovered the long-lost hand of Polycarp. Still encased in solid gold, and not a scratch to be found.

The bloke's mum had indeed stashed the precious relic in her home, erecting a special shrine for it even. And according to her testimony, which I would learn later from Nicky, her ear troubles evaporated. Coincided with the day she took the relic from her son for safekeeping, which led me to believe perhaps she was in on it more than Jozif let on.

Understandably, Nicky was gobsmacked. Not only in the apparent role an eighty-year-old ailing woman played in the disappearance of an important cultural artifact. But also in its apparent, mystical qualities. Of course he thought it was all rubbish. Nothing but the power of suggestion and the ravings of an old hag.

I wasn't so sure. Given my tenure at SEPIO with the Order, I had seen things that no one would believe. Had experienced supernatural occurrences that could only be attributed to the Lord and my faith.

"How did you know?" Nicky asked, walking me back to the front.

I shrugged. "A hunch."

"A jolly well damn good hunch, I'd say!"

"Well, I had help. A good team to carry me across the finish line."

"That's a team I'd want to be on any day of the week."

He grinned at me, the air seeming to rise with a familiar charge.

Until it didn't.

I leaned forward and pecked him goodbye on the cheek. For old-time's sake.

He returned the favor, taking a bit too long in my book, but it was still an innocent goodbye.

"Nice seeing you again, Bourne."

"You too, Nicky."

"Perhaps we'll do it again sometime?"

I laughed, turning to leave. "Not until hell freezes over!"

"Stranger things have happened!"

Don't I know it...

Leaving behind the Hague in a car personally summoned by Nicky, I couldn't help but consider the legacy of Polycarp. The stamina and fortitude it took to face down the powers that threatened the Church, and then go to the grave for his faith— by fire, no less.

Retracing our steps back to the airport, the sky clearer now, with a rainbow lancing across the horizon, a passage from the Book of Acts sprang to mind. In chapter 20, Paul was readying to leave Ephesus for Jerusalem. The Holy Spirit compelled him to go, even though he didn't know what would happen to him there. The only thing he knew for certain was that in every city the Spirit warned him that he was facing prison and hardships.

His answer? *'I do not count my life of any value to myself, if only I may finish my course and the ministry that I received from the Lord Jesus, to testify to the good news of God's grace.'*

Paul and Polycarp. Valuing their faith more than their own lives. May I bear half an ounce of courage as they.

Today was the anniversary of my grandpappy's beheading. And all I wanted was a pizza.

But silly me. Apparently them things aren't a staple of Italy!

Rain was beating against the newspaper held over my head, soaking my sleeve and not doing a lick of good. Still was dripping down my mug, with the distinct taste of Italian ink. Tangy and coppery, and definitely not the tomato sauce and meat and cheese my stomach was aching for!

"Can't a guy get a piping hot pepperoni and anchovies pizza in Rome?"

"Salerno!" Dude at the food truck shouted at me with upraised hand, flat and very Soprano.

"Same difference."

"No! I no make pizza. That American crap food!" There was that hand again, slicing up and down like he was about to chop my head off.

To be honest, I thought he just might, with those bare blade hands of his!

"Watch your mouth, pal. 'Merica is the land of the free and

the home of the ballpark frank that will knock the socks off any pizza from Rome!"

"Solerno!"

"Same difference!"

Now he was slinging God only knew what language at me, rapid fire and probably all curses.

And now wielding a cast iron pan that looked like it meant business!

Time to exit stage left!

Hustling back out into the cats-and-dogs deluge. God just had to rain the funk down on me, on today of all days.

While on pilgrimage to visit the relics of my namesake, on the anniversary of my grandpappy's beheading.

And all I wanted was a blasted pizza!

"What's up with that, Lord!"

It was raining dogs and kittens something fierce now. And I was in the wrong part of town, I just knew it. Just my luck. Lost, wet, hungry. About summed up most of my misadventures in life.

Had taken a taxi into town, but ended up being dropped off in front of some run-of-the-mill city church! Damn cabbie pulled away before I knew what was what. All I was left with was a food truck in the middle of lunch rush hour, surrounded by gray stone buildings selling thousand-dollar purses and cafes with nothing but sandwiches and cappuccinos!

"But no!" I muttered to myself, holding that wilting newspaper over my head—thank God Italians eschewed the digital age, or I'd be soaked through to my skivvies! "I had to traipse halfway across the world on an Order-mandated pilgrimage to get my head on straight, only to find out the land of pizza doesn't sell the dang things!"

My phone buzzed at my leg. I pulled it out of my pocket and answered it with a shout. "Gapinski!"

"Hello to you, too."

It was the chief. I smiled, though I was in this mess because of him.

"Sorry, Silas. In a bit of a mood here."

"International travel will do that to you. Especially to Italy."

I snorted a laugh, spinning around for a gander at my surroundings, trying to find something that would get me out of this mess.

Silas asked, "How you holding up?"

"Tried ordering a pizza, but that was a no go."

"Yeah, they're not really into that sort of thing there."

"Now you tell me!"

"What about Salerno Cathedral? Wasn't it great?"

"Yeah, about that..." I explained about the snafu with the taxicab, and the belligerent food truck dude.

"So where are you?" Silas asked.

"Salerno?"

"Yeah, but where?"

"Haven't a clue! Caught between a food truck and a church place."

"Well, what does your phone's map app say? How close to the cathedral?"

I opened my mouth to answer, then snapped it shut. Hadn't thought of that.

"You did check your map app, right?" he asked with a bit too much snark.

I huffed a sigh. "It's rain cats and kittens out here, I'm so hungry my stomach is eating itself, and I'm in Italy—so cut me some slack, man!"

"How did you become a SEPIO agent again?"

"Ha, ha. Very funny."

Silas chuckled. "I'll get Zoe to draw up some operational plans to get you safely to Salerno Cathedral. Maybe send in your old Marine buddies. Better yet, the Swiss Guard! I'm sure the Vatican can spare a few—"

I killed the call and shoved the phone back in my pocket with a huff. Nearly threw it across the street, but I needed that map app.

So I pulled the phone back out and swiped it to life. Just as a rumble of thunder shuddered from above, and God decided to rain down the funk again!

Threw the newspaper above my head with one hand and thumbed my way through the app with the other. Looked like I was several blocks away. Definitely wasn't gonna hoof it from here!

The rain was rapping against my newspaper like a banshee now, sounding like the snare drums I'd beat on with my garage band as a teen. Called ourselves the Angsts. Heard the word used in my psych class and thought it fit well, given our collective feeling of deep anxiety and dread about our teenage condition and state of the world in general. After all, it was the mid-90s.

Rain was really picking up. Felt less like cats and kittens than water buffalos and rhinoceroses rapping against my newspaper now.

"Come on, Lord, throw me a bone, here!"

A taxicab lumbered to a stop in front of me, a frazzled old couple getting out and asking the cabbie for directions.

"Ask and you shall receive," I muttered as I dashed toward the white car.

About to take back off!

"Wait, wait, wait!" I shouted at the couple. Scared 'em crapless, coming up on them all sudden like. But I couldn't let my ride get away from me!

The gent held the door. "Gracias!"

Sticking my head inside, I asked the captain of this ship, "You free, amigo?"

A large man with a generous gut wearing a black beret and red sweater vest eased around to address me. Swore he looked like Vito Spatafore and worried for a second he'd off me.

"Sure, hop in."

I flashed him my pearly whites and accepted his offer.

"Thanks, pal."

"You American?"

"Yeah, what gave it away?"

"The fanny pack, for one."

I looked down at the faded black pouch bulging at my front side, feeling sheepish.

"Yeah, well, all the cool kids are wearing 'em these days."

"Where to, *tipo*?" the man grunted.

I scrunched up my brow, confused. "Tip? No, dude. Not till afterward. And by after, I mean *safely* after. As in, I'm all in one piece. Comprendo?"

Now he scrunched up his brow, assessing me in a way that made me think he really was Vito Spatafore, and Tony Soprano was about to pop out of the glove compartment and put one in my kisser.

"You heading somewhere, or not?" he asked.

I nodded. "Salerno Cathedral, por favor."

He didn't move, one end of his mouth curling upward. "You'll have to be more specific. Do you know how many cathedrals there are in this city?"

"Uh, let me see here..." I pulled out a piece of paper I'd written the joint down on from Silas's recommendation. "Cathedral of Saint Mary of the Angels—"

"Saint Matthew and Saint Gregory the Great, yeah I know the place. And you're in the wrong part of town, *tipo*!"

There was that word again. I was beginning to think it didn't mean what I thought it meant.

"Just drive, will ya?"

Vito turned around and threw the Peugeot into *'Drive.'* "If you say so..."

The car lumbered out into traffic. Presumably on toward destiny. And hopefully not some warehouse where I'd be dismembered limb from limb! But to the cathedral Silas thought I needed to visit. On this day of all days.

The anniversary of my grandpappy's death.

His beheading, more like it!

That man meant more to me than my own parents. Who were never really parents, but more like wardens in a penitentiary who were too drunk or high to care enough about me to feed me or clothe me or make sure I was in school instead of bummin' around the arcade.

Love me, even...

After things went south at home, Grandpappy was the one who raised me right. Helped me finish high school, just barely. But there he was, in the audience cheering me on with hoots and hollers as I walked across the stage Gapinski style to retrieve my diploma. He helped me navigate the sign-up process to the Marines, and held my feet to the fire and kicked my ass a time or twelve when I wanted to quit. Was there to send me off when I was shipped off to Germany to join the ranks in the global war on terror. Even encouraged me to to join the Order of Thaddeus when Rowen Radcliffe came callin'.

Which was ironic, because the man had died at the hands of Islamic whack jobs during one of the worst missions I'd ever worked for the Order—totally unable to save the man after he'd been rounded up in Israel a few Easters ago.

Today was that day. The anniversary of his death, broadcast on the internet for all to see.

And Silas knew I needed a bit of R&R to process it all. He was the reason I was stuffed inside the tiny, crappy French excuse for an automobile racing through the stone streets of Salerno on toward destiny! Said I needed to get my head on straight, and he suggested communing with the relic bones of my namesake apostle, Saint Matthew. Which I thought was mega-eww, but whatever. Free vaca to Italy, paid for by the Order. Figured I'd get a chance to see a bit of the world without a clock ticking down to no uncertain doom, or getting gunned downed and car-chased by the Church's archnemesis.

Took some doing, but I finally arrived at the cathedral, thanks to my new friend Vito.

"*Qui,*" the cabby grunted from the front, the Peugeot squawking something fierce as he came to a stop.

I looked out between the raindrops streaking my window to find a massive wall with a pair of lions guarding an open gate. Didn't look too impressive. Just a pile of brown bricks streaked by rain, but what did I know. Figured the goods were inside.

"Gracias, amigo," I said, tossing the man a Benjamin for his help. After all, no only was the Order fitting the bill, I didn't want his boss Tony Soprano to come beat me down! Then I headed back into the rain out to meet my destiny.

Newspaper was doing bupkis at this point, so I tossed it in a trash can and ran for cover inside. Only to find a courtyard ankle-deep in water! Hiking it around a stone fountain overflowing with rainwater at the center of green foliage, I made for a set of closed black double doors and barged inside before I floated away. Took some doing, but managed to heave one of them open.

Finding myself standing dripping wet at the back of a massive sanctuary bleached white and lined with rows of black folding chairs with a full-on church service going on!

"Always something..."

The pounding rain rapped from behind. Right before those double doors shuddered with a wicked echo.

Drawing the attention of the priest doing his priestly duty at the front and the rest of the faithful, the service screeching to a halt.

Room turned toward me in one motion. Almost like the

fight scene in the Matrix between Neo and Morpheus, when the two were duking it out and bobbing and weaving all slo-mo like. Even the organ stopped playing, ending on a sour note that seemed to reflect the general mood of the joint.

"Don't mind me!" I chuckled with a wave, voice carrying high above the vaulted ceiling, bouncing off the white and black marble floor. "Just your average American tourist coming to pay my respects to my man Matthew's bones!"

A mumbly rumbled started rippling through the joint now, and scowls and scoffs were being thrown my way.

Above the irritated din a *psst* was thrown up off to the side.

Glanced to my left to find a portly fella with a kind smile and a nice chock of silver hair ringing his bare crown motioning my way.

Glanced to the right to find no one else there, so I figured he must be trying to get my attention.

Pointing to my chest, I mouthed, "Me?"

To which the fella's grin turned upside down and he waved his arms around like he was flagging down a Boeing 747.

Which I gathered was meant for the big beluga who just interrupted the church service.

Me.

I hustled over to the fella and he ushered me into a darkened corner.

"Sorry for the ruckus," I said, shaking my arms dry and slopping rainwater all over the fella like my basset hound! "And sorry for slobbering all over ya, mister."

"Quite alright," he whispered, raising his arms and making a face like I really had slobbered all over him. "Did I hear you say something about Saint Matthew's relics?"

"That's right. Was hoping to spend some time with them. Well, not them exactly. Like cuddling, or anything. Cause that would be weird."

"Quite so..."

"Just wanted to pray by them, ready my Bible and all."

He smiled and motioned with a wrinkly hand, guiding me away from the sanctuary and down a hall of the same bleach white. Not much to look at, and didn't understand what all Silas's fuss was about.

Until I did!

"Holybamoly, Batman…" I muttered as we started down a set of stairs to a room underneath the joint. The place was incredible!

Leading me down a set of stairs, the fella took me into a chapel glowing yellow. Unlike up top, every inch of the place was covered in intricate designs. Whorls they're called, I guess, along with paintings of saints and angels, gold accents. Joint was positively magical. Like Willy-Wonka's fun house, accept without all the candy. Brought tears to my eyes, it was so beautiful. A slice of heaven, that even smelled of heaven!

Oddly, a bit like the ganja I'd tried a time or twelve back in the day, but more earthy and woodsy. Probably incense, knowing my Catholic brethren's persuasion for the smells and bells. But no bells in these parts, nothing else either. Not even a peep of the Mass going on upstairs. Just a calm, peaceful quiet

All of it was just what I need…

"The relics are down at the end." The man said quietly, pointing at an alter, where a stone table stood with tall candles.

"Say, aren't these sorts of saintly dudes patrons of some sort? Like lost causes and toothaches?"

He smiled kindly and nodded. "That is correct. Bankers and accountants is Saint Matthew."

I nodded and thanked the man, then sauntered down to the aisle of dark-wood benches polished to a shiny sheen. He left me to do my thing. Not sure what that was yet, but figured prayer was a good place to start.

Spotting a silver reliquary next to the altar, presumably Saint Matt's bones, I wandered over for a closer look-see.

I frowned, not catching a glimpse of so much as a pinky or tooth chip. "Not much to look at..."

Slightly disappointed, but figured that sitting in the presence of my relics—well, my namesake's apostle relics anyway—figuring just being there was enough, I slumped against the polished dark wood of the first-row bench, the thing throwing up a creek and sagging some under my girth.

I heaved a breath, the air a bit stale, and sighed. Then I closed my eyes and sat still. Or tried to, anyway. Was never much good at that sort of thing and it showed, my legs moving this way and that, and my arms folding and unfolding. How the heck monks sat with the sounds of silence all day, every day, I hadn't a clue. Probably why they drank so much beer! Eventually I settled, and both my limbs and my mind stilled.

"Alright, Lord," I muttered, "why d'ya bring me all the way to Italy? And without the benefit of a large cheese pizza with my name on it?"

Nothing but silence. Not even crickets, it was so quiet!

Figured the Lord's Prayer wouldn't hurt none, so I recited it from memory:

"Our Father in heaven, hallowed be your name. Your kingdom come, your will be done, on earth as it is in heaven. Give us this day our daily bread, and forgive us our debts, as we also have forgiven our debtors. And lead us not into temptation, but deliver us from evil. For yours is the Kingdom and the power and the glory forever. Amen."

Sighing, I crossed myself. Figured that was the way to go in the Catholic cathedral, though I wasn't sure I did it right. Crossing my arms, I felt a bulge at my chest.

That's right! Silas had sent me packing with a Bible, and a note with instructions.

Slipping my hand inside my jacket, I pulled it out.

And frowned.

Thing was wetter than my childhood cat! The black leather

slick with the rain water, and pages edged by crimson splotchy with rainwater.

"Sonofa—"

I gasped with a start. Probably shouldn't finish that in these parts.

Spinning around to make sure I was in the clear, and was, I went with "Always something..." Then I unfolded the note Silas had slipped inside. It read:

Start with Matthew 9:9-13. Then go to Mark 2:14-17. Finish with Luke 5:27-32. Most of all may the peace of Christ that passes all understanding go before you, guarding your heart and mind. Love ya, bro!

I smiled. How touching. Rarely saw that side of Silas, the...what's the word? Affectionate aside. Pastoral, even. Yet there he was, lending me his Bible and guiding me through my reading! What a guy.

I sighed, looking up at the altar and feeling like I was starting to feel the feels from the Apostle Matt. Then I flipped to the first reading. Best get to it.

Pages were wrinkled and creased something fierce. Like the Bible had been well worn over the years. Silas had told me it was the one he'd been given on base in Camp Liberty from a chaplain there after he'd come to Christ, or come back to the faith, or whatever. So the thing meant something to him, and it meant something to me he'd lent it to me for my pilgrimage.

I found my place and read:

As Jesus was walking along, he saw a man called Matthew sitting at the tax booth; and he said to him,

"Follow me." And he got up and followed him.

And as he sat at dinner in the house, many tax collectors and sinners came and were sitting with him and his disciples. When the Pharisees saw this, they said to his disciples, "Why does your teacher eat with tax collectors and sinners?" But when he heard this, he said, "Those who are well have no need of a physician, but those who are sick. Go and learn what this means, 'I desire mercy, not sacrifice.' For I have come to call not the righteous but sinners."

Yep. Familiar. In fact, Grandpappy had read me the story once.

Right after I tried to off myself with that noose that left me dangling on twinkle-toes. After he adopted me official like, he opened up his own copy of the Good Book and showed me this story, how Jesus had taken into his circle of friends someone who was cast off from society. A societal throwaway. Sort of how I'd felt, what with my parents abandoning me to drugs and alcohol. Dude was the lowest of lows in the eyes of the Jewish leaders, a sinner who shouldn't be touched or talked to.

Yet there was Jesus. Not only inviting him to join his crew but sharing a meal with him. And all his other screwed-up peeps! Pictured the dudes and dudettes of my own posse that were decked out in black and eighty-gallon 90s-style goth jeans, smelling like graveyards and looking like 'em too—imagined Jesus sitting down with them and having a beer. Or at least a Dr Pepper, sharing a Big Mac with them, inviting himself over to my house for dinner and a movie with my friends, the lowest of lows in my day.

After all, that's what he did back in the day. Not invite himself over, per se, but he sure as heck accepted the Apostle Matthew's invite to dine with 'tax collectors and sinners' as the

Bible put it. And Grandpappy used that passage to assure me Jesus had called me too. To follow him. That he was interested in me, my life.

Good times...

Now I flipped to good ol' Mark, the next Gospel book on the list. Found my place and read again:

Jesus went out again beside the sea; the whole crowd gathered around him, and he taught them. As he was walking along, he saw Levi son of Alphaeus sitting at the tax booth, and he said to him, "Follow me." And he got up and followed him.

And as he sat at dinner in Levi's house, many tax collectors and sinners were also sitting with Jesus and his disciples—for there were many who followed him. When the scribes of the Pharisees saw that he was eating with sinners and tax collectors, they said to his disciples, "Why does he eat with tax collectors and sinners?" When Jesus heard this, he said to them, "Those who are well have no need of a physician, but those who are sick; I have come to call not the righteous but sinners."

I looked up. There was a difference.

Mark made the point that Jesus was eating and sitting with tax collectors and sinners. That they were his followers, even.

I smiled, chuckling and leaning back in my seat. Pretty much hit the mark on that one. I was the biggest tax collector and sinner you could fine! Well, not tax collector. But like the Apostle Matt, I once worked for the State—hawking my wares to support the whims of a government that was less than stellar. Another reminder that Jesus was on my side.

I flipped to the final section Silas had wanted me to read,

the Gospel of Luke. Figured I'd find the same story. I read:

> After this he went out and saw a tax collector named Levi, sitting at the tax booth; and he said to him, "Follow me." And he got up, left everything, and followed him.
>
> Then Levi gave a great banquet for him in his house; and there was a large crowd of tax collectors and others sitting at the table with them. The Pharisees and their scribes were complaining to his disciples, saying, "Why do you eat and drink with tax collectors and sinners?" Jesus answered, "Those who are well have no need of a physician, but those who are sick; I have come to call not the righteous but sinners to repentance."

Something about the way this one ended struck me.

I flipped back to the other two Gospel accounts, checking with Matt and Mark.

Nope. It ended on a different note.

'I have come to call not the righteous but sinners to repentance.'

To repentance...

Damn straight.

It wasn't just that Jesus was being all kumbaya with the down and out of society. He was calling peeps to repent. To change their life direction.

Peeps like me...

So I did. Spending some time repenting of the bone-headed ways I'd been. To those around me. To God, even. Especially the way I'd blamed him for Grandpappy's death, him not seeming to lift a finger to help him when the man needed him most—especially after devoting so much of his life to him!

But then I remembered what came of it. The man Farhad who had orchestrated it all became a follower of Jesus. Had a vision, a dream, a divine encounter of Jesus himself after it all went down. And then repented of his sins and followed Jesus.

Just like the Apostle Matthew.

Just like me...

Eyes still closed, I inhaled a contemplative breath, stretching out on my bench, the dang thing giving more than I'd like it too.

I recalled after Grandpappy found me swinging from the rope tied around my neck how he explained it all to me from Matthew. Not only how the tax collector had followed Jesus, but why.

'He found what he'd been looking for his whole life,' Grandpappy had said. *'Same for you, Matthew. Jesus is who you've been waiting for your whole life, whether you know it yet or not.'*

Which was ironic. Because I'd been raised in the Church. *His* church, for crying out loud! Yet I never really knew God. Not in the way Grandpappy explained him, opening up his heart to me like that. Explaining there was no way God didn't have a plan for me—still had a plan for me, what with the way my grandpa happened upon me like that. Apparently, Grandpappy felt a tuggin' from the Holy Spirit to visit my house. Which was the only reason he'd come and found me like I was.

I chuckled to myself at the memory—at the *memories*! Then started praying like crazy.

Boy, have I been a jerk, Lord. Blaming you for Grandpappy's death when you used it to bring someone else to yourself. Why could I not celebrate that? How dare I challenge your plan, using the tragedy of my grandpappy's death to glorify yourself. After all you've done for me. After all the ways you've moved in my own story after I tried to end the life you gave me...

But, man, Lord—still not happy with the way it all went down. Grandpappy was the dad and mom I never had! Or at least he was more a dad and mom than my parents ever were. And you took him from me!

Can I be that honest with you?

I waited a beat, not getting any lighting bolts thrown my way, so I figured it was alright.

So I kept going. Pouring my heart out, but also finding peace in the midst of all the—not anger, not really. Frustration. At how my life had turned out. All of it, from my parents to my suicide attempt to Grandpappy's death.

But then I recalled the rando meeting I had with Radcliffe way back when. The time he invited me to join the Order, in a cathedral very similar to this one.

He said, *'God has a plan for your life, Matthew. And I believe it's defending and protecting his Church.'*

Almost lost it then and there at the memory, but I held it together. Eyes brimmed over now, tears dribbling down my cheeks and throat growing tight with emotion.

Felt nice to get it off my chest. What I'd been feeling, how I had been.

I wiped my eyes and sat up straight.

When a noise startled me from my noodling. A gasp, really.

I eased around to find a short, squat man with a small head. Actually, an undersized head. Poor fella's noggin' didn't fit his body. But whatever.

I nodded with a grin and offered a hidey-ho wave.

"It was supposed to be empty."

My grin turned upside down. "Uh, sorry, dude. Didn't mean to rain on your quiet-time parade."

"It was supposed to be empty!" the dude exclaimed again.

Heat ran up the back of my neck. Usually let rando comments from rando dudes in cathedral crypts in Italy just roll off my back. But this dude was really pluckin' my nerves now. It was like the joint was his own personal prayer chapel. Like I showed up and plopped down in his super-fav pew spot. Like—

"It was...*supposed to be...EMPTY!!*"

"Jeez Louise, pal!" I stood and spun around reaching for my backside on instinct, but coming up empty.

That's right. Left my cold, hard steel back home. Couldn't very well take it flying coach! Didn't figure I needed it anyway.

"Pop a squat if you're so eager to commune with the—Holy-bamoly, Batman!"

The fella threw open his oversized coat. Rows of pale brown C-4 blocks were taped to his body with duct tape. Enough to blow up a cathedral!

"Wait a minute..."

He had enough C-4 to blow up a cathedral—

This cathedral!

Filled with a hundred worshippers above.

And Saint Matt's bones a hop, skip, and a jump behind my rear.

Always something...

"And me without my Sig Sauer."

Had to chuckle to myself, too. Because on one of Silas's first missions I'd razed the guy about forgetting SEPIO rule numero uno: Never leave home without cold, hard steel.

And there I was. Pants wrapped around my ankles.

But Uncle Sam trained me well. As did SEPIO.

Time to kick it into high gear. For my sake, and all the peeps still worshiping above.

I took a breath and put out a calming hand. Saw it in a movie once. Figured it was the move to make. Here and now.

"See you've come bearing gifts."

Man didn't say a word. Just huffed and puffed like he was gonna blow down the joint.

Wait. Bad kiddy story reference.

"How about we start with your name, fella," I said, staying put but keeping that hand outstretched, almost like an invitation to come hither.

The man hesitated, licking his lips and swallowing. But he gave it up. "Ermenegildo"

"Armadillo? What is that, Swedish, Norwegian?"

"It's Ermenegildo! And no, Italian. "

I chuckled. "Oh, yeah. When in Rome, right?"

He furrowed his brow with confusion.

"Never mind. Can I call you Ermie? Easier to pronounce, that's all."

He hesitated, shifting on uncertain feet, but then nodded, the tension from his face easing some.

I nodded. "Alright, Ermie, what's your deal? Why the hey-ho day are you packing C-4? Because you don't look like no demolition man."

He chuckled with nervous energy. "No, definitely not."

"Then what are you?"

"Accountant."

"Really?"

"Or, at least I was..." Ermie scowled and clenched his hands into a fist. That's when I noticed the stick capped with a red button, and wires coming from it down underneath his jacket.

The trigger!

Better make a funny quick before the dude goes through with his plan.

"Say, where do accountants live?"

"Huh?"

"Where do accountants live?"

He shrugged. "Where?"

"In a tax shelter!" I laughed and slapped my knee. "Get it? Tax shelter? Man I love that one."

Dude wasn't amused, and he started fiddling with that damn trigger again.

Not good...

"Uh, just a little joke. So, uh, you said *were*."

"Huh?"

"You said, 'Or at least I was an accountant.' What's that about?"

Had to keep up the chit-chat to keep from getting blown to bits.

He swallowed. "I was sacked, that's what."

"Oh, bummer dude."

"Ten years to that damn company, and just like that they sack me, then I lost my health insurance—for me and my family. For my—"

Dude choked over the rest of the sentence and stopped cold. Looked like something had lodged in his throat, like he couldn't breathe. Face started turning red, almost purple. A corkscrew vein started bulging from his head, and it started shaking something fierce.

Then he exploded.

"AND MY DAUGHTER DIED FROM A DISEASE THAT COULD HAVE BEEN FIXED!"

Half expected Saint Matt to get woken up by the man, he shrieked so loud!

"I don't understand," I said. "Don't you have some sort of national healthcare plan here? Thought the EU took care of that sort of thing."

"I am American. Immigrated when my daughter was born. No one would take her with her complicated condition without insurance! She died in my arms in her bed, in our foreclosed house!"

Sounds like I had never heard from a human started erupting from the man. Almost walked over and hugged him, he was so pathetic. And rightly so. Sometimes brute-force capitalism bites.

Ermie recovered, voice suddenly shifting into a growly overdrive. "That's when I knew I needed to get my revenge."

"On Salerno?"

"No! On Matthew!"

Didn't compute at first.

Then it did.

The patron saint of accountants. Of course!

Think fast, Gapinski…

"Hey, listen, Ermie, my man. You don't want to go through with this."

Dude was getting agitated now, shifting back and forth on his feet and clenching that trigger stick of his. Thankfully, thumb off the nuke, but still.

"I know what you're feeling!" I said, trying to empathise with the man.

He laughed. "You ever lose your job and health insurance?"

"No…"

"You have a daughter?"

"Well, no—"

"You ever lose someone so close to you," Ermie shouted again, "that you thought you would literally die of heartbreak?"

"Yes! That's what I'm trying to tell you. And to terrorist whack jobs bent on destroying the Christian faith!"

That seemed to soften the man, his face slackening and even his trigger hand lowering and listening.

I took a breath and swallowed, throwing up a prayer to Saint Matt to come through for me.

On second thought, given the stakes, I threw up a prayer to the good Lord above instead!

Taking a step closer, I said, "Look, the reason I was here with Saint Matt's bones was because I lost someone very close to me as well. A second father—well, more my pops than pops ever was. He was my grandpappy. Err, grandfather."

"Really? How did he die?"

I went to answer, but thought against it, the memory of his head being sawed off burned into my retinas. TMI for such a time as this.

So I went with, "Doesn't matter. What does, is that he was murdered, and right before my eyes."

"Murdered..." Ermie whispered. "Before your eyes?"

His eyes went wide, and that arm went lower. Hand even let go of the trigger.

And that's when I knew I had to act.

For me, yes.

But mostly for all those peeps upstairs. Even that priest who gave me the stink eye when I came barging in on his Mass service.

I took a careful step forward. "That's right. So I understand."

Then another—but just a tad, just a smidge. Didn't want to scare Ermie to death.

Literally. Mine and everyone else's!

"We're the same, you and I," I continued, drawing closer and gesturing to the man whose eyes were locked on my own in some sort of weird trance state. Didn't get it; didn't care. Whatever sealed the deal. "Both losing our loved ones like that. And in front of us, in our face. The world not understanding one lick what it was like."

"Yes, that is true..." Ermie said, mouth slack now.

"So how about we call it a day?" I was sweating buckets with the tension ratcheting up between us. Was within reach now, Ermie an arm's length away. Just a few more—

Something shifted in the dude's eyes. Like when the alien black oil virus ran across all those peeps in the X-Files, their eyes suddenly registering something not of this world.

It was like that, something snapping in Ermie, bringing him out of our connection.

Eyes blinked, then narrowed; jaw snapped shut and clenched tight.

Which meant seconds until he retrieved that trigger stick of his and finished the job.

So I punched him in the face. Once, then again.

Lights out for Ermie.

Felt awful about it, but it did the job.

Ermie folded like a used bathrobe, his hand falling from the trigger and the dude himself slumping toward the floor.

My eyes going wide with the possibility that one right fall could blow the cathedral to kingdom come!

So I slid out a paw and grabbed the front of his jacket with one hand, keeping him upright with all that C-4, then grabbed the trigger stick that started swinging like a bell with the other.

Held my breath, waiting for my own lights-out explosion.

None came.

Blood was seeping down Ermie's face, a geyser of crimson at the nose.

Poor fella. Lost his job, his health insurance, his daughter. No wonder he snapped.

Just glad I was there to stop the lunatic before Italy was the center of another European terrorist attack.

"Can I get some help here!" I yelled, my voice echoing throughout the space I thought of as my own slice of heaven.

The seconds ticked by before my original chaperone came lumbering down the stairs. I explained what had happened, which nearly gave the dude a heart attack! Thought he'd keel over, then and there, but he kept it together and scrambled up top to call the Italian police.

Took a bit, but soon the boys in blue with berets came storming down. Took Ermie off my hands and disarmed the dude, then started slinging a bunch of questions at me in some language I didn't know. Probably Italian, but I didn't pay any attention.

Because it hit me.

I wasn't there for me; I was there for Ermie. Those relics, those martyr's bones had brought us together.

By the providential hand of God, even.

Imagine that...

STORY 4
FORGOTTEN BONES

I woke up to the smell of frying bacon and brewed coffee. And smiled. It was gonna be a great day.

For a few reasons.

Eyes were still closed, and for a minute I forgot where I was.

But then the synapses in my brain connected the dots to remind me where I'd been holed up the past month.

Tunis, Tunisia.

Or, as the ancients would have called the joint: Carthage. One of the former epicenters of ancient Christianity, apart from Antioch and Alexandria, even more than Rome during that day.

That was reason enough to smile. After all, salvaging and exploring dig sites like this one was what I was born for. At least, that's what my uncle Juan had said, God rest his soul.

'*Naomita,*' he would say, '*a Torres is born for one reason and one reason alone.*'

'*And what's that, tío?*' I would say.

'*To conquer. Torres means tower in español. A sign of strength and security, but also surveillance and reconnaissance. The conquistadors of old would make the towers set high on hilltops their home base, allowing them to venture out and slay the dragons of the world.'*

Then he would nuzzle me in all my teenage self—which was not at all appreciated by said teenage self!—and whisper in my ear that I was made to conquer. Just like those conquistadors. He said I was a pillar of strength, of security, that I would survey and reconnoiter the world. Placing my mark on it, my stamp on it, and retrieving from it what needed saving.

Just like today...

I only wished Tío was alive to see it all unfold.

He had passed away the year before and left a massive void in my life. In many ways, an even larger than the one left by my parents when they passed as a teenager thanks to a drunk *idiota*. The man had seen me through those rough years, financed my education in *El Norte*, had hired me on to his salvage and exploration empire—then forgave me and embraced me back into the family when I blew it all to hell.

What he would do to be in my shoes now. To be sitting in a tent baking in the morning sun in some dig site commissioned by the Order of Thaddeus in North Africa, on the cusp of unearthing something that had been buried for over eighteen-hundred years. All of it just waiting to unveil its treasures and mysteries to exploring eyes and minds like mine.

My smile began to fade until a hot breath of morning air gusted in through a flap of canvas to my tent that had come loose in the night—carrying with it the dueling scents of heaven: bacon and coffee.

Nothing tasted better than that pair of breakfast staples. And nothing beat downing strips of fried pig and cups of joe than doing so on a dig site in the middle of North Africa!

I rolled out of my cot, both feet thudding against the cold packed earth with purpose. Which was not only getting a plate of that cooking breakfast, but finishing up the final layer on unearthing whatever lay underneath.

Stepping out into camp, the other tents arrayed around the dig site in an arc on the outskirts of town, a wide blue sky greeted me, sun bright and angled from behind, casting the world below in a shimmering glow and heating it with care as if to confirm the wide-open possibilities that laid before me.

Straight ahead was where that frying bacon and brewing coffee was coming from, a line already forming for the goods with Abraham Patel at the griddle. Piles of gravel and sand lay in bunches around a hole at the center, shovels and rakes sticking out. Sifting stations made of wood frames and strong wiry screens flanked the pit on both sides.

I smiled at the sight. All of it the tools of the trade for any dirt nut like me.

We had been peeling back the layers of time from a long-buried church that had been newly discovered by chance, as these things often are. Some construction company was excavating for a major suburban housing or strip mall project. Forgot which, but it didn't matter. What did was the parish from ancient Carthage they discovered that halted the project in no time flat. It was a minor church, but still one that might hold secrets Christianity could benefit from.

That was the hope anyway.

And today I planned to finish the job.

I sauntered over and got in the grub line. Soon Abraham was handing me a tin mug filled with black coffee and smelling of heaven, then a plate piled high with fatty bacon still shimmering with grease in the morning light, along with a few flapjacks browned to a perfect hue and dripping with melted butter and syrup—all staples of any dig worth its salt, and ones I promptly insisted we spring for.

When I came on board with the Order and was assigned to its SEPIO wing, the project commissioned with taking more overt action to preserve and exploit the memory markers of the Christian faith, I insisted that bacon and pancakes and coffee were standard. Rowen Radcliffe, God rest his soul, balked at the expense, but I worked him over and ground him down to see it my way. After all, it was the least the Order could do for its people spending months isolated from the rest of civilization, getting eaten alive by any number and variety of insects in unrelenting heat and dumped on by random thunderstorm—all while under the threat of marauding terrorists looking for a quick buck through kidnapping Westerners crazy enough to pitch a tent in the middle of nowhere.

So yeah, fatty bacon and syrup-soaked flapjacks and thick black coffee were definitely in order!

I took a sip of the latter, humming with pleasure at the syrupy caramel notes filling my nose with delight as it hit my stomach hard. Which then filled my head with caffeinated delight. The night had been a rough one, sleepless from the mosquitoes buzzing my netting on top of the anticipation from the morning.

"How's it hanging?" I said to Abraham, who was wrapping up his kitchen duty for the morning. Stuffing a forkful of pancakes in my mouth, I added, "Didn't know you were handy with a skillet. Should bring you along on more of these Order digs, these pancakes are amazing!"

He chuckled with a smile and dipped his head, then pushed thick black glasses up the bridge of his nose that reminded me of his counterpart back at SEPIO HQ, Zoe Corbino. "Appreciate the sentiment, Naomi, but I'm not sure I'm cut out for these types of gigs."

"Yeah, I suppose you're more the skinny jeans and latte-drinking type enjoying the comforts of a laptop on an orange beanbag chair in a well-conditioned tech startup than dirty jeans and a T-shirt slugging it out in North Africa."

There was that chuckle again. "Something like that."

"Not that there's anything wrong with that! We need the skinny jeans and latte-drinking type enjoying the comforts of a laptop on an orange beanbag chair in a well-conditioned tech startup saving the world from no uncertain doom. Not least of which is keeping us from getting killed off by our eventual AI overlords."

I was talking too much, and probably offending the poor soul. Always got this way in the heat of a dig, especially on the cusp of the end. And hopefully a big get!

So I shoved another forkful of pancakes into my mouth and downed some coffee, eventually clearing my plate and getting to work. It was gonna be a great day!

Climbing down, I could feel the sand all around me was already reverberating with the heat of the morning sun. It wasn't intense, just hot. Didn't help matters I was surrounded on all sides, but it was what it was. Which didn't matter anyway, because I was about to get my fingers dirty and grow some more calluses peeling back the final layers from the flooring of the church, hopefully resurrecting the ancient Christian edifice for all the world to see.

Took some doing, but with the tools of the trade and several piles of dirt later I managed to clear away the final parts of the floor, revealing magical tiles of indigo and emerald and lavender—all woven into a viny pattern that spread from the center.

And curiously so...

A whistle up top drew my attention. It was Abraham, nursing a cup of Joe. "Magisterial, Ms. Torres. Magisterial work!"

Then there was an applause, the rest of the crew having come around the lip of the pit to offer their congratulation.

So I took a bow, recovering from it with a chuckle and waving them off to get back to it.

"What do you suppose it means?" Abraham asked.

I stared up at him with a furrowed brow, shielding my eyes from the morning sun. "What do you mean?"

He gestured toward the center of the cleared flooring. "The beautiful mosaic of tiles at the center. Looks like a woman about to give birth! In labor, perhaps."

I spun around for a second glance at the flooring, not having noticed the patchwork of those indigo, emerald, violet tiles. Man sort of had a point.

So I hopped up on the ladder for a bird's-eye view.

Astonished at what I saw.

Abraham was right. A woman was prone, lying on her back with a bulging belly, hair flowing around her shoulders and sides over her pregnancy. Another woman seemed to be hovering in wait, as if ready to assist the woman with her natural duty. Cream-colored tiles bordered the mosaic, three deep, clearly highlighting the prominence of the artistic rendition.

Stepping back farther up the ladder, taking in the scope of it all, it made me wonder....

I climbed back down and sauntered over to the center of the mosaic, hand at my chin and eyes searching for something I intuitively knew had to exist. Because that mosaic was just large enough to house—

"*Dios mío...*"

A smile flashed across my face. I knew it! A break in the border. Three of the tiles had come loose. Must have been dislodged during the excavation process. And on closer inspection, it looked like a hollow space underneath!

"Throw me down a light!" I shouted up top. A few beats later, I caught an LED penlight and was on my belly flashing its beam down at the missing tiles.

Sure enough, the white spread down a narrow shaft alongside some other wall, down to the ground beneath.

I breathed in the air coming up from the hole, musty yet sweet, filling my head with all sorts of victorious visions! I would be the next Indiana Jones, unearthing the Ark of the

Covenant—or something like that. Even though my boss Silas said he swore he found it in Ethiopia, but whatever.

There was something down there, that was damn sure.

And Naomi Torres was gonna fish it out.

Shoving off the sandy tile floor, voices swirling in a whispering rush above, I stood and addressed my crew.

"Looks like this thing has turned into something entirely different than we expected." I paused a beat, the air hanging above and around with anticipation. Then I smiled, adding, "We've got something buried underneath these tiles. Something big and made of stone."

A cheer rose above that set my heart on fire. It was a cry of anticipation, of adventure, of hope even for discovering something long-lost that could offer a morsel of insight and truth.

I raised both my arms, trying to quiet them down, but it was no use. So I brought two fingers together and shoved them in my mouth, throwing up a quieting whistle. That did the trick.

"Look, I know this is exciting, but we've got work to do. We're professionals, so let's get to it, alright?"

The crew agreed, throwing up another cheer before everyone slipped into their assigned roles.

First things first, we had to dismantle the mosaic. Wanted to preserve it as much as possible, because it was an exquisite piece of early Christian architecture. Wasn't too often you saw a pregnant woman—or any woman, for that matter—lying prone on the floor of some church! A few of the crew members were experts at that sort of thing, so I let them have at it.

Took some doing, but after a few hours of painstaking, careful extraction, taking care to remove the original mosaic in its entirety without damaging it beyond what was necessary, we had ourselves a hole.

Another hole, down inside the larger one. Nestled down inside was our booty.

There it was. The stone box I had anticipated. Well, not a

box exactly. The sides slanted at even angled down toward the bottom. The top, the crown of what I determined was a sarcophagus, angled upward as well, coming to a rectangular sort of point. It was made of simple sandstone without any markings that I could see from the top.

Which made getting the sucker out of there a top priority.

I immediately got the crew to work. Not that they needed any provoking or cajoling! Unearthing something of this magnitude only came around once in a career, if that.

We spent the rest of the morning setting up the rigging, using some wood beams, rope, and pulleys to construct a hoist that would raise the booty to the surface. Long steel poles were used to help in the extraction.

Took some doing, but soon enough, with enough patience and elbow grease to last us a lifetime, we managed to hoist the ancient artifact out from its grave and onto the tile floor we thought was the main attraction.

Boy, were we wrong!

There was a gasp when the dust was settled, and I immediately saw why.

On the side facing me was the distinct etching of a word.

A name from the look of it.

Perpetua.

Abraham sidled next to me, stroking week-old stubble. "What do you make of it?"

I brought a hand to my chin as well. "Not sure."

"Did you expect this?"

"Nope."

"Then what's our next—"

"Abraham!" Poor fella, biting his head off like that! I closed my eyes and sighed, feeling slightly bad for the outburst, but also not really because the man was crimping my style. "I need space."

I went back to the sarcophagus and knelt, examining the name again as well as the entire boxy object of last repose.

These sorts of things were common during that era, but mostly for those of means. So this woman must have had *mucho dinero*. But it was larger than I would have expected. More the size of a modern coffin, or just a tad smaller, than the sorts of stone edifices to the dead that were typical, which were more like a toy chest than anything.

"Look at this!" Abraham was pointing to the other side.

I hustled to his side, startling at the sight of another name.

Felicity.

Two names on what appeared to be a larger-than-normal sarcophagus, buried under a mosaic at the center of what was presumably a third century Christian church? Forgotten for centuries...

I stood, shaking my head and taking in a stabilizing breath. Trying to clear it from the confusion and set it right. But I knew what I needed to do.

I pulled out my phone. "Time to call this in."

Rang twice before I got Zoe Corbino, director of operational support.

"Yeah?" she answered curtly, the ever-present clatter of a keyboard in the backdrop, the norm for the petite Italian.

Didn't take it personally in the slightest. The woman was a machine providing operational support for us SEPIO agents in the field, juggling a bazillion tasks.

I said, "Zoe, it's Naomi."

"What's shaking, sister?" She seemed less annoyed, but the clattering kept at it.

"Got something here I need to run up the flagpole."

"Uh, oh. Don't tell me Abraham is curled up into the fetal position in his tent again."

I smiled. "No, Patel ain't the issue. And it seems like the guy is actually taking to life in the field."

She snorted a laugh. "Whatever."

"Anyway, is Silas around?"

"No, sorry. He's neck deep with paperwork. Something to do with the board of directors getting their boxers in a twist."

"Nice visual there, *amiga*. How about Celeste?"

"She's about halfway across the Atlantic. Returning from Germany."

I sighed, running a frustrated hand through my long hair that was about two weeks past due for a good washing. I bent in front of the sarcophagus again, eyeing those letters and shaking my head.

Not a clue what or who Perpetua was.

So I asked, "Well, what about Gapinski?"

"Hoss? You must be desperate."

"Now, Zoe, be nice. The lug ain't so bad. But now that you mention it, I'm not sure he's the one to help me out."

"What do you need?"

"Found something in the field that's got me stumped. A sarcophagus we unearthed. Looks old. Real old."

"What about Victor Zarruq? He was some ecclesiastical muckety-muck in those parts for decades. An archbishop, I think."

"Oh, yeah. Silas's babysitter from the board of directors."

Zoe laughed. "Not sure you should frame him like that to either Silas or Victor."

"True. But you think he can help?"

There was more clattering, but she replied, "He seems super knowledgeable about those kinds of real old things. I saw him plant himself in Silas's office earlier in the day, so I could see if he's still there."

"Sure. Why not."

I hadn't had much time with the archbishop, the man spending most of his time consulting Silas and offering his oversight the past year. Took a minute, but she patched me through.

"Ms. Torres," Victor said in perfect English that still betrayed a foreign lilt.

Not that I was judging or anything. I'd spent a decade in the States and still carried the same tell that told the world around me I was not from around here. That I didn't belong, an alien.

"Archbishop Zarruq it's—"

The man offered a corrective *tsk*, sucking in a breath before easing it out through this teeth. Like air escaping a balloon.

"No need for the honorific, Naomi. Victor is fine."

I felt myself blush as I smiled. "Victor, then. Thanks for taking my call."

"The pleasure is all mine, my dear. So what is the occasion for the honor?"

I took a breath, grinning to myself again at the opportunity to explain all that we had discovered.

"I've found something—Well, *we've* found something. My team and I, we all have."

Victor chuckled. A deep, throaty noise that I imagined bubbling up from his generous belly and out through parted lips, his equally generous salt-and-pepper beard jiggling along the way.

"No need to be so self-effacing, my dear. I understand the project in the ancient city of Carthage to be your project. So whatever has been found is *your* find as far as I'm concerned."

My grin widened. I liked this guy!

"Yes, sir." I ran a hand through my hair and turned back to the sarcophagus. "Anyway, we've found something. Well, several things."

"And what is that?"

I catalogued the remains of the ancient basilica, running through the dating findings and the other miscellany before getting to the real reason for the call.

"But the biggest get is a sarcophagus."

"Oh? And who do you suppose it belongs to?"

I knelt before it, running my free fingers across the one name.

"There's no supposing about it. Name chiseled on the outside reads Perpetua."

Thought I heard the phone drop, the clatter was so loud, followed by a string of words in a foreign tongue.

"Victor?" I said into my own phone.

"Forgive me, my dear."

"No worries."

"Perpetua, you say?" Victor said with a gasp. "Are you certain?"

"From what I can tell, yeah. Why?"

"Hers is one of the most famous persecution accounts from the third century. A young woman of considerable means who was slaughtered for her faith in Christ. Her memory has been venerated for over eighteen-hundred years, but here memory markers—that is to say, her *relics* were lost to history."

"Hers and the other, you mean?"

"What do you mean?"

"There were two names listed on the sarcophagus."

"Two?"

"*Si.* Perpetua and Felicity."

The man laughed and seemed to sing out some sort of praise chorus.

"Is that a good thing?"

He chuckled again, deep and from the belly. "Is it a good thing? Yes! For sure it is being a good thing."

"Why is that?"

"Because Felicity was the woman Perpetua's slave!"

Took me a beat, but then I got it, my face widening into a grin and my heart picking up pace.

"Which would mean the likelihood this sarcophagus is anyone else but this early Church martyr is pretty slim."

"Exactly, my dear!"

"Slam dunk, by my standards. And that's official anthropological, archaeological lingo for you."

We both shared a laugh.

"My goodness is this exciting!" Victor exclaimed.

"You're telling me, chief. But who is this *chica*, anyway?"

I could almost see Victor lean back in his chair and prop his hands on his generous gut, getting ready to share his insights like any good teacher, religious or otherwise.

"Well, my dear, Perpetua was a married mother from my homeland."

"Libya?"

"No, from Northern Africa. At twenty-two years old, she was quite the precocious young woman, but she had a father who would hurl insults at her at every stop for her Christianity. He wondered why a woman with such an upstanding upbringing, complete with titles and money and opportunity in the Empire, would reduce herself to a commoner by being a Christian. You see, in those days, status and honor-shame were paramount in those cultures."

"Interesting."

"At any rate, Perpetua pointed out to her father that just as a pitcher of water could be called by no other name, so could she as well be called nothing other than a Christian."

"Sounds like my kind of *chica*, standing up to the patriarchy and all."

"Yours and mine both, my dear. As you can imagine, such talk enraged him, and he attacked her. But the real turning point came when the Empire came for her."

"You mean the Roman Empire?"

"That is correct. Christianity was barely tolerated in the Empire, viewed as another sect of Judaism. But those days began to turn toward a dark chapter in the Church, and she was eventually put into prison, along with a few other fellow believers and her slave Felicity."

I considered this. "The plot thickens. And there we have the link between the two."

"That is true. And that particular local prison of Carthage was a place known for its darkness, and especially for its oppressive heat because of all the bodies pressed in together and sitting near the equator. And that isn't even touching on the cruelty of the guards and their treatment! However, all Perpetua was concerned about was her fellow believers and her infant child."

"Infant?"

"That is correct. She was nursing at the time of her imprisonment. However, thanks to answered prayer, two deacons from the local parish visited her, bearing her child that she might feed him. They even arranged for the infant to stay with her during her prison stay."

"*Dios mío*...But while this travelogue through the woman's history is interesting, can you cut to the chase? I've got a sarcophagus to open!"

Victor chuckled. "Where are my manners? Here is where things get—well, I was going to say good, but that isn't right, is it? How about interesting, for eventually the woman and her companions, including her slave Felicity, were tried before the local magistrate. Her father even came to plead her case after his pleas to her in prison beforehand went unheeded. He tried to get her to recant so she could be set free, but you see he was more concerned for the image he bore by carrying a Christian daughter in his household. He promised never to attack her again for her faith if she would just recant. But you know what she said?"

"What?"

"'*Only that which pleases God shall be done at this tribunal. For know that we are not established in our own power, but in God's.*'"

"That had to piss off her papa nice and good!"

"You could say that, for even during the trial the father berated her and even tried to beat her in public until he was taken away. Yet she proudly declared, '*I am a Christian.*' And so they took her away to be fed to wild beasts. And that is what happened. Which is where the young woman named Felicity comes in."

"How so, Victor?"

"Well, you see, she was eight months pregnant, and she was beside herself that Roman law forbade the torture of women. So she and her fellow prisoners pleaded with the Lord that she might give birth so that she could also participate in their martyrdom at the hands of wild beasts."

"*Dios mío...*You mean she wanted to get tortured at the hands of animals?"

"Precisely!"

"That sure is dedication to the faith." And I didn't know if I would be so bold as to offer the same prayer!

"Three days later, she gave birth to a daughter, paving the way for her to join with Perpetua and the other captives on the day of the public games to die a martyr's death. After continuing their bold proclamation of faith in Jesus Christ, refusing to recant their faith until the end, a martyr named Saturninus was the first victim. A leopard and later a bear would take his life. Saturnus, another of Perpetua's companions, was mauled by a leopard. In fact, there was so much blood that the account said it was the man's second baptism!"

"*Dios mío...*"

"Finally, a wild bull was sent upon the women, which gorged them so. Eventually, the martyrs who were dying from their injuries were lined up to have their throats cut. Each of them, including the dear new mother Felicity, were killed first by the sword.”

“What about Perpetua?” I asked, almost in a whisper now, riveted by the story of fearlessness.

Victor went silent for a few beats, and I swore I heard a few sniffles on the other end.

“Things went differently for Perpetua,” he finally said. “The executioner wanted her to have the experience, the taste of pain. So he thrust a sword into her side. At which point she cried out, the blade doing nothing but injuring her, rather than kill her, for he was quite the novice at the swordsman business.”

“So she was just standing there, spilling blood onto the dirt ground?”

“Yes, until she took the young chap’s hand and plunged the sword into her own neck, finishing the job!”

“Brutal...”

“That is one way of putting it. Another way is *glorious*.”

I twisted up my face in confusion. “Glorious?”

“Yes, my dear, for Perpetua went to her death for her faith not merely willingly, but enthusiastically. Hers was a glorious death.”

Couldn’t disagree with him on that one. And to think, I had discovered the remains of the woman. Her relics. Which would surely fetch a pretty penny on some markets.

My mind suddenly drifted to that possibility, knowing that trading in such religious objects of veneration could fetch hundreds of thousands of dollars, millions even.

But chasing that thought was the shaking finger of my conscience, chiding me at my greedy thoughts at such a time. Especially considering the mess I’d made of my life, and my uncle’s, the last time I’d stepped down that wicked path!

No matter how far I thought I’d come in changing from my past ways, my sinful heart was all-too ready to jump back in!

Like a dark shadow, right there behind me, nipping at my heels and beckoning me to taste from the sour, spoiled well of selfishness.

I sighed, annoyed at the reminder of my past. Then I threw up a prayer to *Jesucristo*, thanking him for his grace and mercy in saving me from my past and for the opportunity to find his faithful martyrs' bones for the sake of restoring the Church's memory markers of these glorious, forgotten women.

"Naomi…" Victor said. "Are you still there?"

I went to answer when a *rat-a-tat-tat* sliced through the afternoon air, followed close by the whine of engines and the screams of frightened men and women.

That didn't sound good!

Que en el mundo?

"What was that sound, Ms. Torres?" Victor said on a shaky breath. "What is going on?"

Had not a clue.

Until I did.

"Naomi!" Victor said again, annoyed now as much as sounding worried.

"Sorry, but I've gotta go. Ten or twelve hostiles just piled into camp, chief. Not sure what you can do about it, but let Silas know and call in the Marines."

Without waiting for a reply, I ended the call then scrambled up the ladder to meet our guests, my Sig Sauer burning at the small of my back beneath my shirt. Knew it wasn't time to break it out for action. Not yet, anyway. But soon enough.

Because whoever these *idiotas* were, they weren't getting a jump on me and my crew.

Or my relics!

Reaching the top, my stomach sank back down the ladder.

Three vehicles, open-top military-grade Hummers skidded to a stop at the one open end of the encampment without any tents, powdery brown dust thrown up and shielding my view of the perps. My crew were fleeing the hostiles, arms raised above their heads and faces strained with fright.

Several more *rat-a-tat-tat*s were thrown into the air and men started pouring from the vehicles. A dozen or more. All dark and bronzed, wearing black and tan shirts and pants, bulging arms carrying heavy weapons.

And they were making for my people! Rattling off more *rat-a-tat-tat*s high into the air and scaring the living daylights out of them!

I went to whip out my own piece and lunge for them, jump into the fray of things, when Abraham clenched by arm. Hand was curled around the butt of my Sig still wedged at my back, and he held it tight.

"Not now," he whispered. "Wait for the moment."

I almost bit back a nasty response about me outranking him and no way in hell would I let some backwater terrorist get the jump on my dig site.

But thought the better of it.

Abraham was right. What was I gonna do, anyway, out-manned and outgunned? Two of the others in my crew had weapons stowed in their tents for security—lotta good that did us—but there was no way they were fishing them out now. So it was me against the dozen whack jobs who just rolled up on us sporting enough machinery and firepower to know they weren't local talent showing off. This was serious.

And it was about to get real.

By now, they had rounded everyone into a bunched group at the center, flanked on all sides by the hostiles. The opening of a door caught my attention, back at the three vehicles.

A man stepped out from the center Hummer. Tall and dark-skinned, with wide shoulders and long dreadlocks piled high on the top of his head like a beehive from hell.

And that's when it hit me.

I knew this man.

Aurelius Chuke...

Which meant I knew this group, who they were with, who they were working for.

Nous!

Two of the goons in black shirts and tan pants hustled toward me, both bearing AK-47s and looking more than ready to use them.

One of the men grabbed me by the wrist and yanked me forward. Abraham protested, but I put out a hand to shut him up—even as I put out another to keep from stumbling to the ground.

Didn't work.

I hit the packed earth hard, my mouth filling with gritty dust, some of it getting up my nose. Knees hurt like a mother, too, but didn't matter. Couldn't show weakness. Not when it was all on the line.

"Easy, easy! I'm breakable!" Abraham complained from behind.

I went to get up when a short, squat soldier jammed that damn Russian-made assault rifle in my ribs, and a familiar laugh was thrown my way—deep, from the gut, at my expense.

The large man I recalled from a year ago of packed muscle in full military fatigues sauntered over, clearly distinguished from his soldiers' brown makeshift uniforms. His head was bulbous, is if it were merely an extension of his neck. Dreadlocks like cords of rope twisted around his head up into a hive that meant business and hung down to his shoulders and beyond the length of his back. The man was African, sub-Saharan, with dark, ebony skin and haunting eyes set behind a flat nose. A jagged scar ran down the side of his face, from his right ear to the corner of his mouth, and his skin was similarly pockmarked with signs of violence.

Me and the rest of SEPIO had run into him and his crew at a dig site very similar to this one months ago—had to have been a year now. He'd taken an important archaeological find relating to Emperor Constantine that turned out to be one piece of a larger confessional code that ended up turning out very different than any of them thought.

Now he was back. On my dig. Again. Presumably to steal more goods I had just uncovered that could be crucial for preserving the memory of the Church's martyrs, inspiring millions of faithful Christians with their story of persecution and death.

Not on your life, *idiota*!

Chuke removed a pair of aviator sunglasses and wiped the lenses with a white cloth, flaring his nostrils before smiling widely, a gold tooth gleaming from the front.

"Naomi Torres. We meet again!"

His greeting was accented by the region's tongue with a throaty baritone. Colonel Gold Tooth was dressed in military garb. However, his shoulders were clear of patches or any other official accoutrements, so he wasn't really military. Just playacting. He had donned his sunglasses again, his face set as flint toward the hole behind her.

I went to stand, not at all OK with the man looming over me and making a go at making a show of confidence—

When I was thrown back down by that short, squat mutt, his AK-47 barrel digging back into my ribs.

I cried out; couldn't help it. The men around laughed, and Chuke chuckled along.

My ears burned as heat raced up the back of my neck at the indignation. My right ribs screamed in pain. The *idiota* probably broke two or three! But I wouldn't give them the satisfaction of controlling me.

So I went to all fours, then to my knees.

Mutt-Man raised his rifle again, getting ready to jab me a second time—possibly right upside the head—when Chuke intervened. Spoke some local-language gibberish to the fella before he slinked away.

"Aurelius Chuke..." I said. "We meet again."

His grin widened. "The one and only." The Nous whack job nodded at me, holding out an open palm to help me stand.

I took one look at it before hocking a good-sized loogie at it and rising to my feet on my own.

That didn't go over well.

Before I knew it, I was back on the ground, one side of my face blooming with pain. Worried my eye would swell shut and nose would burst with blood from the smack, but both seemed to hold steady.

"You insolent fool!" he growled. "I wouldn't be so daring, Ms. Torres. Not with the lives of your precious crew members on the line."

I looked up to find the goons rounding them up. And Mutt-Man with his AK-47 jammed into Abraham's back.

Poor fella was whimpering something fierce. Everyone was.

I muttered a curse in my native tongue under my breath and made a decision I hoped I didn't regret.

Putting those moves I'd learned while serving in the Israeli Defense Force way back when—mama having been a native-born Israeli before marrying papa, and I taking up the charge to serve at eighteen—in one move I whipped out the Sig Sauer still nestled at my back and pointed it at Colonel Golden Tooth's face.

That got their attention.

Pronto!

All weapons seemed to train on me as one. Mutt-Man even let go of Abraham, who scurried away to the other crew members and pleaded with me to surrender.

Chuke just laughed, the man folding his arms and grinning at me, that golden tooth glinting again in the sunlight.

"Impressive, Ms. Torres. But let's dispense with the theatrics and put away the weapon. You're outgunned and out-manned. Surely you know you'd lose in whatever fight you put up."

I tightened my grip, aiming for dead-center tooth.

"Yeah, well, at least I'd blow that damn tooth clear through the back of your skull."

Got him to flare his nostrils at that one. And drop his arms in a huff, the man narrowing his eyes at me and the golden tooth disappearing in a closed-mouth grimace.

Then he raised an arm and snapped his fingers, calling something out in his native tongue until a man appeared.

Dragging Abraham by his arm.

"Surrender now," Chuke said, "or I blow his head off."

My breath went out from me, but I didn't give up. Tightened my grip and focused on that bulbous head of that Nous whack job instead of the Indian man about to lose it.

Perhaps literally.

I swallowed, answering, "You wouldn't dare. Not with your life in my hands. You shoot him, I—"

Before I could finish, Chuke was withdrawing a pistol and discharging it.

Sending Abraham crying out and to the ground clutching his leg.

I didn't return the favor. Instead, I froze. Stiff at the sight of blood oozing between his fingers down onto the pale brown dusty ground and the sound of his moans.

"Flesh wound, Ms. Torres," Chuke said, refocusing my attention to the bastard. "Next time he won't be so lucky. Now, be a good girl and surrender."

Checkmate.

I let go of the butt of my pistol, and it swung loose at the trigger guard on my finger.

He grinned. "Good girl."

Mutt-Man promptly relieved me of my weapon and grabbed my arm, yanking me toward Colonel Golden Tooth.

"That is not being necessary." He said something in his native tongue, and the goon loosened his grip, sauntering to Chuke's side.

"What do you want, *bastardo*?" I growled, neck hot from the heat of the day and the heat of the moment.

"I am not speaking Spanish, but I take that as an insult." He pointed to the hole in the ground. "We've come for whatever it is you've uncovered below."

"Down below?" I asked with surprise. "Nothing but a dusty old church floor."

"And a box of ancient bone relics, from what I understand."

I let a gasp seep, disbelieving Nous could have already heard of our discovery.

Chuke chuckled, that annoying tooth gleaming at me with mocking pride. "Don't be so surprised, Ms. Torres. By now you should know Nous sees all, hears all, knows all. Besides, you didn't imagine this level of archaeological excavation would escape our notice, now did you?"

I went to throw back a smart-ass retort, but clenched my jaw tight.

Qué pesadilla...

This is like the Emperor Code nightmare all over again, when the same clown rolled up and ran off with a key piece of Church history. But what could I do?

Drawing out his pistol again, Chuke motioned toward the ladder leading down to the bottom of the hole. "Let's move. I believe the bones of a certain Carthaginian martyr await."

I hesitated, but then saw Abraham lying on the ground, blood soaking the dirt beneath, though it looked like he had staunched it with a torn shirt. So I relented, climbing around and slumping down the stairs below, drilling the man with eyes I wished could kill.

Didn't take long before I reached the bottom, and Colonel Golden Tooth and Mutt-Man were joining in on the fun.

Reaching the bottom, Chuke whistled from behind, walking out in front and eyeing the sarcophagus before kneeling before it. "Quite the specimen of Church history. Perpetua. I know the story well."

I snorted a laugh and crossed my arms. "Yeah, right. And what's your interest in it, anyway? Not like it's part of some grand religious conspiracy to bring down the Church."

"Perhaps not some conspiracy to bring down the Church, but certainly one chink in her memory to protect her."

"How so?"

"A brave woman. A brave mother, no less, willingly dying for her faith. Such heroism would wreak havoc with our plans."

"What plans?"

There was that tooth again, at the front of that grin. "Time will tell. All you need to know is that allowing these relics to see the light of media attention would infuse too many with too much inspiration. And inspiration to faith is the last thing Nous needs."

I didn't entirely understand what he was talking about, what plans he was speaking of and all. Silas sure might. But what I did get was how such a witness could inspire others to offer the same devotion to Christ in the face of persecution.

"Enough talk." Chuke waved his pistol toward the stone box. "Open it."

Everything within me wanted to rush the man. But I relented, knowing my stupid act would get everyone else above killed.

Grabbing a trowel and a hammer, I got to work loosening the mortar that had sealed the lid shut. Took some doing, chipping it piece by piece in order to still maintain the integrity of the box—after all, it was still a precious piece of history. My inner archaeologist couldn't let it go.

Soon I was finished, and we were good to go.

Setting the tools of the trade down on the tile floor, I

grabbed one side and looked at Chuke. "Help me with this, would you? Grab the other side and listen to my instructions."

He threw me a grin, but obliged. "Yes, ma'am."

Instructing him on how to wiggle the lid back and forth, we eventually managed to wrench it free from its hold.

"Moment of truth," Chuke said, eyes wide with anticipation.

I nodded and gave the final heave that sent it to the floor.

My stomach leapt with anticipation as the lid slid down and away.

Right before it sank to the ground beneath.

Damn...

"Empty?" Chuke said with disbelief, leaning over the stone box and gripping its sides with open-mouth surprise.

I leaned in for a closer look, but he was right.

Nada.

I leaned back and shook my head. "Lost to history, I suppose. Not a surprise, given the age of the relics. Thieves could have taken them half a millennium ago—even a millennium ago."

I sighed. Partly in relief, partly in equal disbelief—disappointment, even. No way would I have wanted something as precious as the relics of Perpetua and Felicity to fall into the hands of Nous. But...damn, it would have been nice for the Church to have their bones as memory markers for their witness to their faith in Christ unto death.

Chuke stiffened, shaking his head with a chuckle. "As empty as the memory it supposedly held."

Then he turned and sauntered back to the ladder.

I said, "What, that's it? Just like that, you're gone."

He shrugged and called back, "We came for the relics. Nothing more."

Motioning to Mutt-Man, he climbed the ladder as his goon trained his rifle on me. Then he turned around and shouted down, that golden tooth glinting at me again: "But I'm sure we'll meet again soon, Ms. Torres! Until then..."

He threw me a wave and spun around from view, Mutt-Man hustling up the ladder after him.

The sound of car doors opening and engines roaring to life filtered down to me from above as I stared at the sarcophagus again, catching my breath from what had just went down—but also still disbelieving the truth of the matter.

Empty...

Just an oversized box filled with nothing but dust and stale air.

Which was a shame.

Any *chica* who would stand up to the powers that be and lay down her life for her faith without question—she was the type whose memory needed to be preserved. Needed to be broadcasted for all the world to hear!

As they drove away, I stared at the empty box. A box with at least the names of two women that memorialized their testimony of whole-hearted devotion to *Jesucristo*.

While their bones had gone missing, their memory sure hadn't. And I pledged to make it known. These women would no longer be forgotten.

Not only by sharing my discovery and their story.

Their martyrs' memory would live on in and through me, through my life and my witness.

Even unto death.

STORY 5
REBEL'S BONES

I took a drag from my cigarette and blew the spicy haze into the overcast night, stealing a glance behind to make sure I was in the clear.

White light cascaded down not from the moon, hidden behind a canopy of thick rain clouds, but from large work lights erected around the site. Gave me away if anyone was looking, but I didn't care. Needed the quick fix, for a variety of reasons, but especially this night, on this operation.

Torres was still laid up in bed with the stomach flu. Gapinski was still doing his thing with the backhoe. Celeste looked to be supervising.

So I leaned against the high stone wall, white row houses with sloping red roofs on the other side throwing up earthy smoke into the waning evening. Then took another drag, holding it a beat before huffing the haze out into the night. Perhaps the chimney smoke would mask my bad habit and keep me from the wrath of the missus-to-be.

The nicotine sent a soothing jolt through my tongue, the refined Perique tobacco grown in Louisiana, aged and fermented in oak whiskey barrels. Pack said it's organic, but whatever. As long as it sent my tastebuds dancing and the synapses of my brain humming with delight.

Another drag, more dancing and humming.

Did the trick, in spades.

Holding the smoky haze from a habit I'd picked up in Iraq and kicked a time or two, I blew it out into the night again, the grunting protests of a digger reminding me of the stakes. For me, for the Church.

With my career as Master of the Order of Thaddeus hanging by a thread, I needed a win. A no drama win. Without car chases and gunfights, without drones blowing up buildings or terrorist whack jobs offing Christian martyrs.

The kind of win this night was meant to hand-deliver on a silver platter. Had all the permits in order, not resorting to stealing this time around. Everything on the up-and-up in a church cemetery in North Ockendon, the easternmost and most outlying settlement of Greater London, housing the remains of one of the Church's unsung heroes.

William Tyndale.

The Christian martyr was a long way from the site of his demise, Vilvoorde, Flanders, a Belgium province that had seen his torturous death. He had been betrayed and handed over to the Holy Roman Empire where he was strangled and burned at the stake in the Flemish town.

But his story didn't end there. Or so I hoped...

For the better part of a month, I had been searching for his remains, tracking them down to the Greater London parish. I wanted the Church to know this man, to memorialize the one responsible for connecting people to the heart of God in ways no one had been able to before.

I inhaled again and closed my eyes, the nicotine-laced smoke doing wonders to help me make it through the final leg of the mission.

"Not another fag, Silas!" groaned Celeste, coming in from stage left.

Dang!

I jolted from the wall and flicked the butt out into the grass, trying to hide my sin. Worked about as well as when I had tried to stash the Sports Illustrated swimsuit addition under my Army-issued mattress when pops barged into my room on a base in the South Pacific—catching me red-handed gawking at Tyra Banks.

Didn't work then; definitely didn't work now.

Celeste came up and put her arms around my waist. "Caught you red-handed, mister." She nestled her nose against my back and breathed me in.

Then promptly coughed and choked like she was dying.

"Caught is right," she moaned, stepping back. "Oof, you smell like the chimney from the terrace house I grew up in!"

I turned around and threw up my arms. "Guilty as charged."

She tilted her head and smiled, Gapinski still grunting up the way with that digger of his. "You must be nervous if you're resorting to prior bad habits."

I pulled my jacket close and sniffed the night air, that earthy smoke a fine stand-in for the spicy tobacco, stalling to answer. A night wind whipped through the town square riffling the herring-bone wool open, carrying with it the trace scents of roasted meat and onions, sending a chill down my neck as I hemmed and hawed.

But then I thought, what's the use? We were engaged, soon to be married, so why hide it?

So I looked her in the eyes and nodded. "That's about the long and short of it."

She drew closer now, wrapping her arms around my waist.

"But why? Everything is in order. You worked your Silas Grey magic on those ecclesial administrators, convincing them of the cultural value of exhuming Tyndale's bones and putting them on display for the world. It's all gone without a hitch. Now it's just us SEPIO agents and a backhoe. What could go wrong?"

I laughed and raised a brow. "What could go wrong, really? Have you worked a SEPIO operation in the last few years?"

She giggled. "I suppose you are right. But you've been a real champ this whole mission retrieving Tyndale's memory." She paused, turning toward me now and brushing a stray lock of hair blowing in the wind behind an ear. "This doesn't have anything to do with the Order board of directors, does it?"

I looked to the grass, green and lush from the early spring rain, white clovers speckled throughout, averting her eyes at being exposed. Never did like that feeling, the world knowing what I was feeling, what worried me. Maybe it was life as a military brat, having to put up walls a mile high just to survive. Maybe it was my pride at wanting to appear that I had it all together, never needing help to solve my problems. Maybe a little of both.

"I suppose so," I admitted, kicking at a stone.

She took my hand. I looked into that face of hers, delight and assurance rising.

"No way they'll sack you after delivering your coup de relique."

I laughed. "Coup de relique. Relic blow. Nice."

"Thought it carried a nice ring to it. At any rate, cheer up, Charlie," she said with a grin. "It'll be alright. It always is."

Cheer up, Charlie...

I smiled at the song title she often quoted from *Willie Wonka and the Chocolate Factory*.

I went in for a kiss—

When Gapinski shouted, "Stop your snogging. We've hit the mother load, chief!"

Throwing me off my game and causing me to startle back into position.

"I'm going to kill that little bugger," Celeste complained

before wrapping a hand around my head and pulling me in for a nice one.

"Get a room..." Gapinski muttered in the distance.

We both laughed, putting stray hair behind our ears out of nervous habit.

She said, "Suppose we should see this through."

"Yes, suppose so. Sounds like we've hit pay dirt."

"Or something more, with Gapinski at the helm."

Hand in hand, we walked across the lawn leading to the site where Gapinski had been working that digger. Reminded me of the many archaeological digs I had been on, the ones I'd supervised even. Except this wasn't digging up the past that had been forgotten so much as it was unearthing the past that had been memorialized.

Had tracked down an unmarked grave to the parish church in the small English town. Originally had poked around a monument erected in 1913 by Friends of the Trinitarian Bible Society of London in Belgium, a bluestone thing that had stood as a memorial to the man who was the Father of the English Bible, but that didn't pan out. It was merely erected at the site of his death, rather than marking out Tyndale's burial site.

So I continued looking, poking around in the annals of history. Until I came to the plot of last repose in the cemetery Gapinski was grunting around inside with that digger in hopes of proving his bones had survived, and then exploit them for the sake of the Church.

A plot that had been unmarked, but really wasn't. To the discerning eye.

While his name wasn't listed on the centuries-old tombstone, Tyndale's last dying words were.

'Lord, open the king of England's eyes!' the Father of the English Bible had shouted as a last prayer before he passed from this life to the next.

One thing led to the next, and now I found myself walking

back to the church cemetery where Gapinski looked to be finishing up unearthing the remains of a martyr who meant more to the Church than she knew.

While we in the twenty-first century take for granted the myriad of English-language Bibles available to read, whether for personal devotion or corporate worship or study, such wasn't always the case. There was a time when the average English-speaking person couldn't read the Bible in their own native tongue.

The Catholic Church in particular was to blame for that, requiring the Word be read and spoken in the officially sanctioned Vulgate translation of the Bible, going all the way back to Saint Jerome who translated the original Hebrew and Greek manuscripts into Latin. The Church, especially the Latin variety that spread across much of Europe, saw to it that it and it alone was the only Good Book read and studied by believers.

William Tyndale changed all of that.

Born around 1494 in Gloucestershire, England, William Tyndale studied first at Oxford before completing additional studies at Cambridge. From there, he served as chaplain to Sir John Walsh of Little Sodbury and tutor to his grandchildren, where he had this growing desire to offer people, his people, a new translation of the Bible. But not in the officially sanctioned Latin, but instead into the common English of the common people of his day.

Inspired by John Wycliffe's translation of the Vulgate into Middle English and Martin Luther's new German translation that similarly sought to connect the Bible to the common Germans, Tyndale wanted to similarly offer God's Word in the vernacular of the English people. Ambitious as it was, he proposed the project to Cuthbart Tunstall, bishop of London, but he was less enthusiastic, refusing to neither fund nor sanction it. Around 1525, he travelled to Wittenburg, Germany, where he began the process of translating the Bible into

English on his own, using Luther's Bible as a model for what he would eventually produce for his own people.

A year later, in the spring of 1526 fresh copies of Tyndale's New Testament translation, as well as the first five books of the Old Testament, the Pentateuch, landed on the English shores—alarming Bishop Tunstall and many other ecclesial figureheads. So alarmed was the bishop, he personally bought up all the copies to prevent the everyday person from getting their hands on something not officially sanctioned by the Church. Which had the ironic effect of funding Tyndale's second edition!

Some of the controversy of Tyndale's Bible arose from how the man translated certain words and phrases. Mostly, the concern stemmed from the threat the new work posed to Roman Catholic ecclesial control, as well as the ability of the everyday Christian to read the Bible in their own English language. So severe was the reaction that his translation was banned from the Church and from England. The controversy grew so severe that he was forced to flee to Belgium for refuge from not only the Bishop of London, but King Henry VIII himself.

And that was where his journey ended. On October 6, 1536 Tyndale was sentenced to death by strangulation after having been found guilty of heresy for translating the Vulgate into the common English of his people. He was eventually burned at the stake, and his remains were disposed of.

Where was never entirely clear, though I had found a remark from John Foxe, in his eponymous *Foxe's Book of Martyrs,* that had been the key he had been waiting for: *'William Tyndale, being in the town of Antwerp, had been lodged about one whole year in the house of Thomas Poyntz, an Englishman, who kept a house of English merchants.'*

"Thomas Poyntz of North Ockendon..." I muttered,

recalling my research as we entered through a gate in the dry-stone walls older than I cared to imagine.

The man had been part of a family of merchants who had inherited the family manor and lands at North Ockendon, and other parts of south Essex, on the death of his brother John in 1547. Although the details of transfer of ownership was murky, given the right was first granted to his sister-in-law after John's death, and many had wondered whether he had in fact inherited the estate, I had found evidence suggesting he had.

Thomas Poyntz was particularly interesting to the story of Tyndale, because he ran a lodging house for English merchants in Belgium—where William Tyndale stayed. It was also the place where he was arrested for translating the New Testament. Although a strong supporter of Tyndale, Poyntz narrowly escaped being burned at the stake himself, fleeing back to England where he took up residence in the family estate.

Confirmation that Thomas did then live at North Ockendon was given by a certificate of residence issued to the collectors of tax in London. Dated February 1556, it read: *'Know ye that Thomas Poyins of North Ockendon in the said county of Essex esquire is assessed within the said Hundred of Chafford wherein he doth dwell.'* Evidence for his residing in North Ockendon and actively managing the estates was also found in a surviving document from an action brought against him by one Jane Warren, apparently concerning her tenancy of lands in Upminster and North Ockendon.

At some point, his children all arrived in England, one of which was Gabriel. Sir Gabriel Poyntz, who also happened to be buried inside the church. Gabriel inherited the family estates, and later he was knighted and served as Sheriff of Essex. A memorial at the North Ockendon church states that Thomas Poyntz 'sleeps...in this chapel' although it appears he was buried elsewhere. The memorial is a reminder of the peril in which Gabriel's father found himself through his support of

Tyndale. Although Thomas Poyntz escaped Tyndale's burning-at-the-stake fate as a heretic, his suffering was prolonged, being caught up in religious and political currents by his determination to help Tyndale in 1535.

The connection between Poyntz and Tyndale is what brought me to the church east of London, and the unmarked gravesite I was sure was the place of last repose for Tyndale.

"I'm through!" Gapinski's voice pierced the darkness, sending a jolting ping of excitement coursing through me.

I squeezed Celeste's hand and threw her a grin.

"We're through!" she said.

I nodded and ran back to ground zero, with my fiancé in tow.

Just as Gapinski was climbing down from the digger anchored to the backend of the cemetery, a hole in the ground of mawing blackness promising good things to come.

"So we're in?" I asked, letting go of Celeste's hand and hustling now, heart banging away in my chest and head.

He mopped his head with a red bandana, a wicked heat having hung around the grounds late into the night. "We're in.

"Any trouble?" I asked.

"No trouble. But this place gives me the creeps."

"Aww," Celeste said, slugging the man in his shoulder, "Gapinski's afraid of a cemetery full of ghosts?"

"Naw, it ain't like that," he replied, swiping that rag down his eight-ball head and down his neck now. "A helicopter has been circling in the distance."

I nodded, coming to the edge of the exhumed burial plot. "Yeah, I heard that. Apparently, there's been a string of burglaries in the area."

"All the more reason to get the heck out of Dodge."

We stood around the plot, a modest white limestone sarcophagus inside with a patina of green algae and creepy crawly things set against its brilliance.

I took a breath, praying to the good Lord above that the goods I'd been seeking the past few months were nestled down inside. I needed a win. Strike that: the *Church* needed a win. But I'd be pleased to swipe a crumb from the table of the Church's feast.

"Can I just say," Gapinski said, "isn't it a bit odd we're digging up a Protestant Reformer who defied the Roman Catholic Church, only to venerate him as a relic?"

"A memory marker of the Church," I corrected.

"Tomato, potato. It's all the same, isn't it?"

Celeste crossed her arms. "Bloke has a point."

"Funny you should say that," I said, "because Tyndale actually had a pretty robust view of relics, and really all ornaments, signs, sacraments, holy days, and ceremonies of the Church."

"You don't say," Gapinski said. "Like, the man was down with worshiping relics?"

"Not worshiping, per se. Here, let me..." I took out my phone and flipped to some saved research I had, pulling up the piece I myself found intriguing. "Here, listen to this..." I read:

If, for an example, I take a piece of the cross of Christ, and make a little cross thereof and bear it about me, to look thereon with a repenting heart at times when I am moved thereto, to put me in remembrance that the body of Christ was broken and his blood shed thereon for my sins; and believe steadfastly that the merciful truth of God shall forgive the sins of all that repent, for his death's sake, and never think on them more; then it serveth me and I not it; and doth me the same service as if I read the testament in a book, or as if the preacher preached it unto me.

"So he's saying," Celeste said, "as long as it serves some higher purpose, relics of any sort, like these martyrs bones here, can be spiritually healthy?"

I nodded. "That's right. But he goes on..." I read further:

And so, if I make an image of Christ, or of anything that Christ hath done for me, in a memory, it is good and not evil until it be abused. And even so, if I take the true life of a saint, and cause it to be painted or carved, to put me in remembrance of the saint's life, to follow the saint as the saint did Christ; and to put me in remembrance of the great faith of the saint to God, and how true God was to help him out of all tribulation, and to see the saint's love towards his neighbor, in that he so patiently suffered so painful a death, and so cruel a martyrdom to testify the truth, for to save other, and all to strength my soul withal and my faith to God and love to my neighbor, then doth the image serve me and I not it.

"Well how do you like that," Gapinski said, shaking his head. "A Protestant defense of relics. Grandpappy would be turning over in his grave, especially coming from the likes of Tyndale!"

I laughed. "And that ain't all his defense. Check this out." I found my place again and read:

Neither to kneel down before an image, in a man's meditations, to call the living of the saint to mind, for to desire God of like grace to follow the example, is not evil. But the abuse of the thing is evil, and to have a false faith, as to bear a piece of the cross about a man, thinking that so long as that is about him, spirits shall not come at him, his enemies shall do him no bodily harm, all causes shall go on his side even for bearing it about him; and to think that if it were not about him it would not be so, and to think if any misfortune chance that it came for leaving it off, or because this or that ceremony was left undone, and not rather because we have broken God's commandments, or that God tempteth us, to prove our patience, this is plain idolatry. And here a man is captive, bond and servant unto a false faith and a false imagination, that is neither God nor his Word.

"Alright, I'm sold!" Gapinski said, spinning back to the digger to retrieve something. "I'd say we get cracking."

He returned with nylon straps, handing them over to me. I nodded, then jumped down into the maw of darkness, landing hard on the limestone lid.

I offered a hand to Celeste. "Care to join? Two hands are better than one, as the Good Book says."

She grinned, taking my offer. "Thought you'd never ask."

We got to work securing the straps around the limestone box. Took some doing, and more time than I'd liked, but we managed it. Tossed the ends up to Gapinski before hauling ourselves out of the pit.

He secured them to the digger's arm then finished the job, bringing the machine back to grunting life and working his magic.

Slowly, surely, he started raising the dead to life.

"Easy..." I said, putting out a staying hand.

Gapinski ignored me, keeping his eyes on the ball until it surfaced and he eased it down to the ground beside the mawing pit.

My stomach went with it, an adrenaline rush sending butterflies soaring inside my gut.

I ran up to its side, the limestone coffin holding up surprisingly well.

"They sure don't make them like they used to," Celeste said as I ran my hands across its surface.

"I'd say," Gapinski said, coming up from behind.

I inhaled a stabilizing breath, the pungent aroma of earth dizzying as I took in the moment, disbelieving months of work was paying off.

"Well, shall we?" The man was holding up one of the shovels, ready to jam it into the narrow crack running along the coffin's upper edge.

"You know..." I said, heart racing now in anticipation but feeling like I should say some words before we got to it. "Tyndale was largely responsible for us English speakers having access to the Bible. Something like ninety percent of the King James Bible is Tyndale's, did you know that?"

"Fascinating," Celeste said.

"Yeah. A regular Jeopardy Daily Double," Gapinski quipped. "Now can we get to it?"

Ignoring him, I said softly, "*I have here translated brethren and sisters most dear and tenderly beloved in Christ,*' Tyndale wrote in the Prologue to his finished edition, '*the new Testament for your spiritual edifying, consolation and solace: Exhorting instantly and beseeching those that are better seen in the tongues than I, and that have higher gifts of grace to interpret the sense of the Scripture, and meaning of the Spirit, than I, to consider and ponder my labor, and that with the spirit of meekness.*'"

Brought tears to my eyes quoting the man who had given me access to God's Word.

"That's beautiful," Celeste said.

"Yeah, a real turn of phrases, that Tyndale was." Gapinski held up the shovel again. "Now can we?"

I smiled, grabbing my own shovel. "Let's do this thing."

Took some doing, but we managed to scrape away the mortar holding the lid tightly to the base of the Medieval coffin. Then we levered the top with our shovels until we got our hands under both ends.

"Moment of truth..." Gapinski said, waving his eyebrows at me with a grin.

I nodded. "Moment of truth."

Then we lifted, hoisting the top up from the coffin, a musty breath of death escaping from inside as we laid it on the ground.

The three of us peered over the edge.

"Blimey..." Celeste said.

"What the..." I responded, heart sinking to the ground beneath.

"Was Tyndale a transvestite?"

"Gapinski!" Celeste said as I reached inside toward the body lying in repose.

Dressed in—well, a dress! And it's features fully intact. Leathery with decay, but definitely not charred to a crisp as a stake-burning would have rendered them.

"I don't get it," Gapinski said. "What gives?"

I spun around, leaning against the limestone box, head spinning. "What gives is I was wrong."

Definitely not Tyndale. Not in the slightest!

"Then who is this?"

"Who knows." I sunk to the ground now, the earth soft and wet against my jeans, but I didn't care.

Celeste offered, "Probably some lass who fancied Tyndale's dying words. Or had the same opinion as he of the monarchy."

I was so close. How could I have messed this up so bad?

Silence hung over the cemetery, but for the distant thwapping of rotor blades from that damn helicopter searching for burglars and a chorus of crickets and tree frogs serenading me while I wallowed in my stupidity.

An arm wrapped around my shoulders. Celeste's. "Sorry, love. Valiant effort, though."

Another arm wrapped around my other shoulder. Gapinski's. He sighed. "Yeah, chief. What she said."

"Thanks…" I said, muttering a disappointed curse under my breath before turning around to my knees, their arms sliding off my shoulders.

I put my hands at my back and stretched out the frustration, staring up into the darkened sky. How could I have missed this? It all made sense. The connection to Poyntz and North Ockendon. Catching sight of the original tombstone lying on a pile of dirt, I slumped back down beside it, tracing the faded words with my finger.

'Lord, open the king of England's eyes.'

I sighed, shaking my head. "The freakin' grave marker held the guy's last dying words…"

Gapinski plopped next to me. "Apparently he wasn't the only one who wanted the King to see."

"Guess so."

"Why'd you pick this guy, of all guys, to go after?"

I sat firmly on my bottom now, the cold, wet dirt sort of a nice way to wallow. "Suppose I appreciated the man's boldness to buck the system, you know? Both political and religious. Going to the mat to please God, rather than man. Working hard to help connect regular, everyday people to the heart of God by handing them their own copy of the Bible."

Celeste sat next to me now, leaning her head on my shoulder. "I imagine every English-speaking Christian owes Tyndale a bit of a debt."

"Got that right. Did you know many of the famous phrases from our English versions we take for granted, the verses even we all know and love were thanks to Tyndale?"

"Really? I had no idea."

"Get out of here," Gapinski said. "Like what?"

"Like the most famous verse in all the Bible."

Took them a minute, but they said in unison: "*John 3:16?*"

I chuckled. "That's right." Then I quoted: "For God so loveth the worlde yt he hath geven his only sonne that none that beleve in him shuld perishe: but shuld have everlastinge lyfe."

"Not the Vacation Bible School verse of the day I remember," Gapinski said, "but close enough."

"Thanks to his Bible translation," I went on, "Tyndale has also been credited with coining the word *atonement*, a word often used to describe Christ's death for our sins and its application to our lives, paying our price in our place. Then there are several phrases from his translation that have made their mark on our English Bibles—English culture, even."

"Such as?"

"Like *'let there be light'* for a start, from Genesis 1. Then there's *'my brother's keeper'* from the Cain and Abel story in the same book. The Nativity story of Jesus' birth has *'it came to pass'* and then three doozies from Jesus' teachings: *'seek and ye shall find, ask and it shall be given you;' 'judge not that ye be not judged;'* and *'the signs of the times.'*"

Celeste gave a marveling sigh. "I had no idea how far into the English language Tyndale had infiltrated."

"All thanks to the dude's Bible translation," Gapinski said with as much marvel.

"That's not even the complete story," I said, "Not only did he impact the English language, his translation would go on to impact future translations in the English language. The Great Bible of 1539, the Geneva Bible of 1560, and then the biggie: the King James Version of 1611."

"Get out of here!" Celeste said.

"The King James Bible." Gapinski snorted a laugh. "So he's

the dude I have to thank for my childhood misery memorizing verses before I could have a bowl of ice cream."

I nodded. "That he is. In fact, some have suggested that he himself was the unrecognized translator of the Authorized King James Version, the most influential Bible in history."

"Blimey..." Celeste said. "I suppose the Father of the English Bible is an apt nickname."

Taking in a breath, my head filling with the faint traces of the earthy chimney smoke in the distance, and my tongue tingling for the spicy taste of an American Spirit. I held my head in shame at losing the trail of the relics of the man who the Church needed as a reminder of all it had thanks to his courage.

Almost had him...

Well, I thought I did. But I'd been duped. But it made sense! Thomas Poyntz had been Tyndale's most ardent supporter. His son memorialized his father with a—

I sat up straight, eyes widening. "Memorial..."

Then I stood and took off toward the church, Gapinski and Celeste throwing up confused protests from behind. Didn't care. I wanted into that nave to see something I should have seen to begin with!

Coming up fast, I grabbed the knob painted black to the door of the Church of Saint Mary Magdalene, the steel cold to my hand and unyielding.

Locked tight.

But when did that ever stop me?

Pulled out a utility knife with a lock pick inside. *Semper Paratus* might be the Coast Guard's motto—always prepared— but I fancied it as a life goal for myself. *Sua Sponte*, the motto of the Rangers wasn't bad either. Of their own accord. A term of law describing an act of authority taken without formal prompting from another party.

Exactly.

Like picking a lock to a church I guaranteed was hiding the relics of an English martyr inside.

I heard a click just as my teammates ran to my side.

"Oy, Silas, love," Celeste said, gulping down a breath. "What are you doing bloomin' breaking into a church?"

"What she said," Gapinski said, sounding even more winded than her.

I threw them a grin. "I'll show you."

Door opened on well-oiled hinges into a modest nave smelling of old wood and stone. Like the Princeton library where I had spent way too many Friday nights as a professor, which was probably why I was single. It was stuffy, the heat cloying and clinging with humidity. Darkness shrouded the wood pews dutifully lined in neat rows facing the front, a vaulted ceiling throwing up shadows at my phone's flashlight in a way that sent a chill down my spine.

Now to find what I came looking—

I spotted it. Off to the side. A pair of marble statues lying in repose, hands praying and at their chests and prone over generous marble sarcophaguses. The monument sat in front of a series of six coat of arms underneath a canopy of blue. Sir Gabriel Poyntz and his wife. Next to it was a memorial to his father.

I smiled, wiping my forehead slick with sweat but not caring a lick. "There it is..."

"There what is, love?" Celeste asked, sidling up to me with crossed arms. "What are you playing at, Silas?"

"Look!" I pointed to a plaque and read: *'Thomas Poyntz—for faithful service to his prince and ardent profession of the evangelical truth suffered chains and imprisonment in regions across the seas plainly already destined to be killed except he himself trusting in divine providence looked for a miraculous escape from prison.'*

"It's a memorial to some dead dude," Gapinski said. "So what?"

I scoffed. "Not just any dead dude. Tyndale's patron! And there's his son." I shuffled over to the ornate sarcophagus. "Thomas's son."

"Now that's mildly interesting," Celeste acknowledged.

I threw her a grin, "I thought so."

"Still doesn't give you the right to go barging into a church in the dead of night."

"Yeah, man," Gapinski said, shaking his head. "Bad juju. Besides, what are we going to do? Break into another tomb?"

Celeste said, "He's right. The grave outside was one thing. We had permission for that. But this...What are you expecting to accomplish?"

I shook my head. "I don't know..."

I showed my light around the top of the edifice, searching for something that would give any indication Tyndale was interred in—

Then I saw it. The familiar phrase.

'Lord, open the king of England's eyes.'

Bingo.

The others saw it too, the pair gasping together.

"And look!" I pointed at clear lines that looked like some sort of compartment plastered over at the base of the sarcophagus.

"I'll go get the shovel," Gapinski said, running back outside.

Another minute, he was back, and we were chipping away at the border. When that didn't work, I finally grabbed hold of the shovel and smashed the thing myself. Celeste threw up a panicked protest, but I didn't care.

And it worked.

My act of vandalism revealed a compartment with a box inside. Made of wood and perfectly preserved.

I took a breath and threw my teammates a grin. "Moment of truth."

Celeste leaned in. "Do you really think..."

"Only one way to find out." Gapinski was grinning now and gesturing at the opening.

So I got to it. Took some work, but eventually I slid it out. A long thing, running most of the sarcophagus's length.

Removed the lid and found a perfectly preserved skeleton, bones looking a bit charred, with a silver plaque affixed to the skull, leaving no doubt as to whom these bones belonged to.

William Tyndale.

"Blimey..." Celeste said.

Gapinski swallowed. "What she said."

There they were. I'd done it. Found what no one else had found.

And it felt damn good.

A thwapping came in the distance, throwing up an irritation at the back of my brain with the thing ruining my moment of glory.

"That damn chopper is back..." I muttered, still marveling at the set of bones nestled down inside with preservation in that box.

Gapinski smirked. "Malls must close early in these parts if crime is that bad to call down the boys in blue from above!"

I nodded, returning to the box, grasping the sides and confused at how it felt.

It was vibrating. Ever-so-slightly, but it was there. And getting more pronounced. Must be from that bird outside, which meant it was close. Sure sounded like it.

I stood, looking at the ceiling and really feeling the bassy vibration now.

Something about it felt familiar. Seemed off. The timbre and tone sounding less like something the boys in blue were tracking down burglars.

And more like the boys in fatigues might be bearing down on our position!

Celeste looked toward the ceiling too with a furrowed brow. "Sounds like it's nearing."

Then snapped her head in my direction. "Us..."

"Damn straight it is."

"Always something..." Gapinski growled, whipping out his Sig Sauer from behind his back.

"Steady..." Celeste said, bearing the same weapon, both hands wrapped around its grip and looking around. "Last thing we need is to cause an international incident, and bearing illegal contraband."

I pulled out my own weapon now—Beretta, a holdover from my Ranger days—and looked it over, confused. "What do you mean, contraband? You mean our weapons?"

Celeste frowned. "No, those bones you stuffed back in its hidey-hole. Of course I mean our weapons! Handguns were banned a few decades ago, after all."

"Always something," Gapinski growled again. "And you better tell those whack jobs coming in hot and heavy about your crazy Brit rules!"

He pointed out the window.

My stomach sank even as my heart jolted forward at the sight of four hostiles shimmying down ropes swaying in a whipping wind from above.

Are you kidding me...

I grabbed the textured black rubber grip to my Beretta nestled at my back and slid it out. Always something is right.

Just like that, the hostiles were on the ground. And moving into position.

Then moving toward the cemetery.

I edged to a window facing the south lawn still lit up like a Christmas tree, the figures making quick work hustling toward what looked like our hole, being careful to avoid the light but also not really caring.

Celeste sidled up to me, the dueling scents of lavender and

vanilla offering a calming breath to the madness. "Clearly they seemed to have come for the same goods."

"Clearly."

"From this angle," Gapinski said lowly, crouching at my other side, "them are some pretty sophisticated grave robbers."

I grunted a laugh. "You think?"

Coming up to the mawing void, the hostiles assembled around the opened casket we'd left behind, peering inside and looking like they caught the meaning of what we'd found.

And then they seemed to catch the scent of our trail—all four pivoting toward the church and fanning out, making for the entrance.

Didn't help matters that blasted wood door was wide open!

I stood. "We didn't close the door!"

Gapinski snorted a laugh. "We? What's this *we* business?"

Celeste joined me. "No, love, *you* didn't close the door."

"I was through first!" I hustled down the aisle of pews, taking in the lay of the land and searching for cover. On the double!

Gapinski was close behind. "Don't think the four whack jobs care who opened the door."

Followed by Celeste. "But they sure will be interested in why it's open!"

We three shuffled behind a knee-high stone wall at the choir loft behind a massive wood pulpit, slumping low against it.

Just as white lights flashed inside. Tactical weapon mounts. Which meant these boys weren't no joke.

Or messing around.

Two took the door on either side, leaning in one at a time to confirm it was clear, as far as they were concerned.

Then a lead stepped in, crouching low and hustling to the first row of pews.

Followed by another, who made for stage left. Then one of

the others, aiming stage right. The other stayed at the door, light spraying back out into the light for cover at their six.

It's what I would've done, back in my Ranger days.

Shoot. It *is* what I did back in my Ranger days!

SEPIO held still, crouched low against the stone wall and biding our time.

Light swept the nave, and a I chanced a peak

Catching sight of the lead turning toward the Poyntz sarcophagus.

That's when I saw what we'd done wrong.

What *I'd* done wrong!

I whispered. "We didn't hide the bones!"

Gapinski shook his head. "There you go with that *we* business again..."

Celeste flashed me wide eyes, shaking her head in silence and telling me all I needed to know.

Not good...

The two other hostiles quickly followed their lead, the three coming up to the wood box. One flipped the lid to find what we'd discovered. Looked close to grabbing and dashing.

Which meant I needed to do something.

Pronto.

Had an idea, so I told Celeste and Gapinski about a set of light switches I'd spied behind me when I took cover. Could be useful, lighting the place up and catching them by surprise, lighting them up to let them know what was what.

Was about the only thing we could do short of coming out shooting. Something I wanted to avoid. So the pair nodded and got ready, the three of us agreeing to only maim, not kill. That is, if we could help it.

I got into position, then let her rip.

Flipping the switches, the place bloomed with yellow light.

Clearly catching the goons off guard.

Gapinski and Celeste sprang to their feet.

Just as the two wing men to the leader whipped their weapons our way and sent up a *rat-a-tat-tat* spray.

Bullets went high and wide and cut short after the pair—my SEPIO pair—sent *pop-pop-pop* rejoinders of their own.

Their shots sinking into the hostiles' shoulders, who weren't wearing any heavy protection.

Beretta extended, I made for the lead goon. "Hold it there, partner! Not another move."

Gapinski and Celeste backed me up, pivoting to the fella still at the entrance, giving me cover and keeping him at bay.

Didn't take long before I was facing the man who was carrying the case with both hands. Tall, wide-shouldered, all neck with face masked and his weapon slung around his shoulder.

I threw him a grin. "I'll be taking that, if you don't mind."

"What? This?" he grunted.

Before tossing it in the air.

On instinct, I went to my knees and caught it just before it smashed against the stone floor. But in the sudden move, my weapon slipped from my hand and skittered across the floor.

Both of which were what the goon wanted.

Free from the box, he nailed me in the side of the head with his knee.

Sending me backward, and the box tumbling from my grip.

Gapinski and Celeste were busy with the other hostile still at the entrance.

So that left me and Lead Goon to wrestle over Tyndale's remains. And wrestle we did.

Back and forth, tumbling over one another. Kicks and punches to the gut, and swipes at the head.

Until I recovered my Beretta, kicked Lead Goon square in the chest, and aimed dead-center mass.

"It's over," I said, lungs searching for breath after the workout.

"I wouldn't do that if I were you..."

My breath seized in my chest at the sound of a voice I knew all too well.

Sebastian!

I faltered my grip at the thought.

Which gave Lead Goon whack job the window he needed to land one in my jaw and send me staggering to my backside, weapon skittering across the floor.

Celeste and Gapinski were aiming for the other hostiles, who had recovered and were aiming with as much intent. My goon was standing over me with the wood box and aiming at my head.

And Sebastian was now standing over me with a smirk I wanted to slap off from here to kingdom come.

But I held it together. Wincing, I sat and rubbed my jaw. "You've grown out your hair since the last time I saw you."

He laughed. "And apparently you've taken up the nasty habit of smoking. Could smell you a mile away."

I stood now, coming face to face with the man I hated on earth most of all. My mouth tasted coppery, blood seeping in from the corner from a cut.

"What are they, Camels, Marlboros?" he asked.

I sent bloody spittle to the floor, inches from his foot. "American Spirits."

"At least you've got taste."

I glanced around the nave. None of this looked good.

Celeste and Gapinski were still training their weapons on the two goons, who equally had them in their sights. Lead Goon was recovering Tyndale's remains. The goon at the entrance was figuring out how to be useful.

Classic stalemate.

"What do you want with this?" I growled, drilling my brother with hateful eyes.

Knew I shouldn't bear such an emotion toward him, toward

anyone. Couldn't help it, after all he'd done, after all we'd been through.

Sebastian shrugged. "Same as you. Master William Tyndale, Father of the English Bible. What a memory he bears, gifting the world's number one spoken language with access to the Good Book. And martyred by those who would keep the people from encountering God. Makes for a good story. One I'm sure you'd leverage with gusto."

"How did you find us?" Celeste asked from across the way, Sig Sauer still aimed at her man.

"A well-placed mo—" he stopped short, nearly spilling the beans. But he didn't. Instead, that smirk returned. "As they say, never kiss and tell…"

He turned to Lead Goon, saying, "Now, Ian, if you'd be so kind as to hand over the remains…"

The man shoved past me and gave Sebastian the wood box.

Sebastian threw me a smirk. "It's been real, Silas." He went to turn away.

But I clocked Lead Goon in the temple, then again, dropping him cold.

Then clamped a hand down on the box. Real good and tight, so that the little punk couldn't leave.

Sebastian smiled and yanked hard.

No go.

His face fell now, and he pulled harder, his jaw getting into the action.

I matched him grip for grip, yank for yank.

"Silas, if you don't—"

He went at it again; so did I. Back and for we went, no one from either side lending a helping hand with the stalemate.

A sound at the door caught my attention as Sebastian I played tug-of-war with the box, the bones rattling inside with desecration.

Even as a muffled shout and thudding struggle was thrown up outside.

Then someone appeared silhouetted in the door.

"Not so fast, *idiota!*" a pistol blast echoed across the nave, a bullet sinking into the floor a foot from Sebastian.

He froze. Box in hand with wide eyes. Just like he'd looked one summer when I caught him trying to sneak that same Sports Illustrated swimsuit edition out of my room.

Busted.

And by Naomi Torres!

"I thought you were sick in bed, sister?" Gapinski said. "Stomach flu and all."

Torres shrugged. "Was restless lying in bed watching reruns of the Bachelor. Wanted in on the action. Looks like I came at just the right time."

I'd say. Except we were back to the stalemate.

Torres's gun was trained on Sebastian, with one of his men taken out at the entrance, the lead one still unconscious at my feet. Celeste and Gapinski each had a Nous whack job in their sights, who were taking aim at my SEPIO agents.

Not good...

Sebastian and I held our grips on the box of Tyndale's bones, eyes locked on one another but the truth of the situation beginning to dawn on each of us. More him than me. So I went for it.

"Here's how I see it," I began. "You can let go and get the heck out of Dodge."

"Or?" Sebastian said through clenched teeth, eyes narrowed and a corkscrew vein bulging at his forehead.

I shrugged. "Or, you die."

He smirked. "Cute. But so will you."

"I'm the only one who's not in someone's aim. So no. I won't."

"Way to throw us under the bus, chief!" Gapinski said.

"And Torres, I suppose." I tightened my grip and narrowed my gaze. "Either way, you lost. The box is mine. So we can stay like this or let the sparks fly. Or I suppose wait until the rector of the church appears in the morning to find us all standing around with our pants at our ankles. Then things will get real interesting."

"I won," Sebastian said through gritted teeth. "I had you all. I had *you*."

I laughed. Couldn't help it. Threw up a shade of crimson across his face, that vein popping even more, but I didn't care. My brother had become more absurd.

"You think this is about you and me?" I said. "It's not. Not even close. What I do is for the Church. For my faith. What you do..."

I shook my head, disbelieving the conversation. "What you're doing is about you. About Sebastian. Always has been, ever since you left the faith. I know what happened to you, the demonic abuse and how it severed any interest in the Church. I'm still sick about it all. So I get why you broke away. But now, it's like you don't even want there to be faith. Don't want there to be a God even, one you're responsible to. And you don't want anyone to believe in him either, in Jesus Christ."

I paused, taking a breath, but finishing my thought. "So no. What you do is about you. What I do is about others—serving their faith, protecting their faith, defending their faith. As well as God."

Sebastian's face hardened, crimson rising to purple now until I thought he would lunge at me with the fury of decades of pent-up rage.

But he didn't, his face slackening and one end of his mouth curling upward. And then he did something I didn't expect.

Letting go, he leaned in with a devilish gaze I thought was the horned nightmare himself. "This ain't over, big brother..."

Then he snapped his fingers. "Call the chopper. We're going."

He spun around and hustled across the stone floor, brushing past Torres with his two Nous goons grabbing their downed man still lying at my feet like any good soldier.

The thwapping of chopper blades returned as I looked at Celeste, who shrugged but held firm her grip, both her and Gapinski and Torres keeping the Nous whack jobs in their sights.

I held the box with both hands, a rattling inside catching my attention. Heart leaped at the sound, thinking Tyndale was coming alive inside! Until I realized my arms were trembling, the adrenaline rush giving way.

Sebastian and his goons slinked outside and into the awaiting bird, the wind whipping leaves and dirt around the property, along with his long blond hair in a way that made him look like a crazed version of myself with my own long locks, but dark brown.

I supposed that was true, the evil twin to my better angel—or so I hoped.

Soon the bird was lifting into the sky, and my brother disappeared into the cloudy night.

"Until the next time, baby brother..."

The sound of the chopper soon faded, and I was left only with the clamoring cymbals of my thoughts—how much I despised Sebastian, how little I understood how things had gotten that way, how much I wished they were different.

That he was different. That we were, as brothers.

As family.

An arm wrapping around my waist startled me, bringing me back to the moment. But I knew the truth of the matter. My family had been dead a while, only to resurrect into a new kind. The Order, my SEPIO teammates. And soon the woman at my side.

Another hand slapped my shoulder and gave it a squeeze. It was Gapinski. "Sorry to see your weaselly little bro back in the saddle of things. Hope it didn't get you down."

"Yeah, chief," Torres said, sidling up to Gapinski. "Don't waste a minute on that piece of work, regretting his blood-ties and all."

I chuckled, touched by their gestures. "Don't worry. I'm not. And thanks to you, I'm alive to tell the tale, along with making sure Tyndale's bones are given proper recognition."

"*No fue nada!*" she said, swatting a dismissive hand. "Nothing at all."

Gapinski snorted a laugh. "Not sure that dude with the bloody face you clocked would agree!"

"Probably not!"

"I must say," Celeste said, resting her head on my shoulder, "that was a close one. Closer than we've come in a while."

"Yeah, but we've got our martyr's bones," I said. "Kept them out of the hands of Nous. That's what's important."

Torres scoffed "Just barely."

"In our line of work, I'll consider that a win."

"But what do you make of the effort?" Celeste asked. "To care that deeply about the bones of some obscure English martyr? What do you make of it?"

"And did it sound to you," Gapinski added, "that the dude was about to say some mole clued him into our whereabouts?"

Celeste took a breath and folded her arms. "Yes, he did."

"What's that about, chief?" Torres asked. "You believe him?"

Now I took a breath and folded my arms. "Not sure. Either what it's about or whether to believe him. But knowing my brother...I wouldn't put it past him."

"To bury a mole," Gapinski said, "inside the Order?"

I said nothing, considering the implication.

Which was too horrifying to think about.

That nighttime wind came back, along with its chill. I drew

my coat up around my neck, face hardening as I stared into the darkened sky, heart growing harder toward the only one left from my family. The one who had not only betrayed me at every turn, but who had apostatized completely from the faith he had once been in love with.

I sniffed at the air, the spicy, earthy scent of a collection of fireplaces wafting across the field. Reminded me of the pack of sticks nestled at the inside breast pocket of my coat. Wanted nothing more than to pull one out and light up, inhaling deeply of that same spicy tobacco—those earthy scents combined with the sweet tang of nicotine to set me back on track.

But I didn't.

Not just because Celeste would have been disappointed, my fiancé encouraging me to pursue better habits. But because I wanted to rely on the Holy Spirit instead of the pack of American Spirits.

This was a fight, a continued fight. Not merely with the flesh-and-blood hostels the Order of Thaddeus had become familiar with over the years. It was a war with the principalities of this dark world to contend for the once-for-all faith. To protect the memory markers of that faith. Whatever they might be. Whether they be images, relics, ornaments, signs, or sacraments, holy days, ceremonies or sacrifices. As Tyndale had said, they are for our service—the Church's service, to offer us an example, to raise our gaze heavenward, to reorient our lives around the eternal.

Finally I said, "You said earlier what I made of Sebastian and Nous's effort."

"That's right, chief," Gapinski said. "What do you make of it, all of it?"

I shrugged. "Why does Nous—why does my *brother* do the things they do? They want to destroy the memory of the Church. However that memory manifests itself. By any means."

"Including stuffing a mole inside our ranks," Celeste said.

"*Dios mío...*" Torres groaned.

"That's right." I spun around and looked my teammates square in the eyes. "But we won't let that happen, will we—whether it's destroying the Church's memory of our faith or infiltrating the Order with some Nous agent in our midst?"

"No way, Silas," Celeste said, smiling at me with a nod.

"Not a chance!" Gapinski exclaimed, folding his arms with a nod.

Torres snorted a laugh and shook her head. "Is it really a question?"

A grin spread across my face. "That's the spirit."

Now it was our turn to leave, heading to the black Mercedes GLS that sat anchored in the church's parking lot. We lived to fight another day—literally, thanks to Torres, and Gapinski and Celeste.

My team.

The Church's defenders.

And with a box of martyrs bones as a consolation prize.

Not a bad night.

ENJOY THE RELIC ADVENTURES?

Thanks for joining SEPIO saving the memory markers of the Church! Each of these characters are heroes in my *Order of Thaddeus* series. If you've missed the adventures, start today:

Holy Shroud • Book 1
The Thirteenth Apostle • Book 2
Hidden Covenant • Book 3
American God • Book 4
Grail of Power • Book 5
Templars Rising • Book 6
Rite of Darkness • Book 7
Gospel Zero • Book 8
The Emperor's Code • Book 9
Strange Blessing • Book 10

Enjoy the story? Here's what you can do next:

If you're ready for another adventure, you can get a full-length novel in the series for free! All you have to do is join the insider's group to be notified of specials and new releases by going to this link: www.jabouma.com/free

You might also like my apocalyptic sci-fi thriller series, *Ichthus Chronicles*. Set 100 years in the future, the last remnant of Christianity is threatened from forces inside and outside the Church, written in the vein of the *Left Behind* series. Start the adventure today: www.jabouma.com/books/apostasy-rising-1

If you loved the book and have a moment to spare, **a short review is much appreciated.** Nothing fancy, just your honest take. Spreading the word is probably the #1 way you can help independent authors like me and help others enjoy the story.

GET YOUR FREE THRILLER

Building a relationship with my readers is one of my all-time favorite joys of writing! Once in a while I like to send out a newsletter with giveaways, free stories, pre-release content, updates on new books, and other bits on my stories.

Join my insider's group for updates, giveaways, and your free novel—a full-length action-adventure story in my *Order of Thaddeus* thriller series. Just tell me where to send it.

Follow this link to subscribe:
www.jabouma.com/free

ALSO BY J. A. BOUMA

J. A. Bouma believes nobody should have to read bad religious fiction —whether it's cheesy plots with pat answers or misrepresentations of the Christian faith and the Bible. So he wants to do something about it by telling compelling, propulsive stories that thrill as much as inspire, while offering a dose of insight along the way.

Order of Thaddeus Action-Adventure Thriller Series

Holy Shroud • Book 1

The Thirteenth Apostle • Book 2

Hidden Covenant • Book 3

American God • Book 4

Grail of Power • Book 5

Templars Rising • Book 6

Rite of Darkness • Book 7

Gospel Zero • Book 8

The Emperor's Code • Book 9

Strange Blessing • Book 10

Silas Grey Collection 1 (Books 1-3)

Silas Grey Collection 2 (Books 4-6)

Silas Grey Collection 3 (Books 7-9)

Backstories: Short Story Collection 1

Martyrs Bones: Short Story Collection 2

Ichthus Chronicles **Sci-Fi Apocalyptic Series**

Apostasy Rising / Season 1, Episode 1

Apostasy Rising / Season 1, Episode 2

Apostasy Rising / Season 1, Episode 3

Apostasy Rising / Season 1, Episode 4

Apostasy Rising / Full Season 1 (Episodes 1 to 4)

Apocalypse Rising / Season 2, Episode 1

Apocalypse Rising / Season 2, Episode 2

Apocalypse Rising / Season 2, Episode 3

Apocalypse Rising / Season 2, Episode 4

Apocalypse Rising / Full Season 2

Faith Reimagined **Spiritual Coming-of-Age Series**

A Reimagined Faith • Book 1

A Rediscovered Faith • Book 2

A Ruined Faith • Book 3 (2020)

A Resurrected Faith • Book 4 (2021)

Mill Creek Junction **Short Story Series**

Get all the latest short stories at: www.millcreekjunction.com

Find all of my latest book releases at: www.jabouma.com

ABOUT THE AUTHOR

J. A. Bouma believes nobody should have to read bad religious fiction--whether it's cheesy plots with pat answers or misrepresentations of the Christian faith and the Bible. So he wants to do something about it by telling compelling, propulsive stories that thrill as much as inspire, while offering a dose of insight along the way.

As a former congressional staffer and pastor, and award-nominated bestselling author of over forty religious fiction and nonfiction books, he blends a love for ideas and adventure, exploration and discovery, thrill and thought. With graduate degrees in Christian thought and the Bible, and armed with a voracious appetite for most mainstream genres, he tells stories you'll read with abandon and recommend with pride—exploring the tension of faith and doubt, spirituality and culture, belief and practice, and the gritty drama that is our collective pilgrim story.

When not putting fingers to keyboard, he loves vintage jazz vinyl, a glass of Malbec, and an epic read—preferably together. He lives in Grand Rapids with his wife, two kiddos, and rambunctious boxer-pug-terrier.

www.jabouma.com • jeremy@jabouma.com

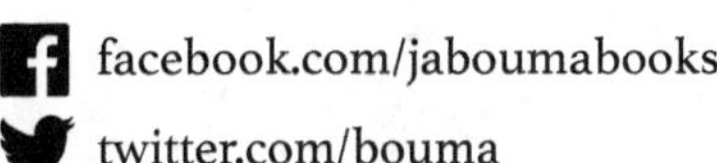
facebook.com/jaboumabooks
twitter.com/bouma
amazon.com/author/jabouma